Who Little Johnny Gill?

A Victorian True Crime Murder Mystery

KATHRYN McMASTER

If you enjoyed reading this book check my website for new titles at www.kathrynmcmaster.com and please leave a review on the Amazon website.

This book is dedicated to my father, Danby Maitland McMaster Steel, who had a passion for true crime stories, which has led me to have a fascination for this subject for over forty years.

ACKNOWLEDGEMENTS

First and foremost, I would like to thank my editorial team who helped shape the manuscript. For my lovely book cover, I have to thank my book designer, Hayley Faye.

To the British Newspaper Archives, I would like to express my gratitude in granting me permission to use their collection of newspapers and images that provided the framework for the story.

To all my beta readers and members of my very valuable launch team, your support has been invaluable. Thank you for all your time and effort dedicated to the cause! You have all been amazing!

Finally, a big thank you goes to my husband, Philip Bax for his love and continued support for nearly 35 years in allowing me to follow my dreams and reach my aspirations. To my dear friend of 50 years, Linda Steel, who followed the progress of my book very closely, and not least, sincere appreciation goes to my eldest son, Kent, who took control of the marketing and the Kindle conversion.

Without the help of everyone concerned and their enormous generosity in donating their precious time, this book would never have been possible.

CHAPTER ONE - THURSDAY 27TH DECEMBER 1888

Forests of mill chimneys pierced Bradford's skyline. Soon they would be belching forth their daily toxic plumes, poisoning the air of the masses in exchange for riches of the few. Gas lamps cast pale, faint shadows onto the doors of the tiny back-to-back houses where workers had started to stir. One by one, doors opened, disgorging both old and young into the darkness, into the swirling smog. Humanity, drowning in poverty, hunched up in thin winter coats and shawls, snaked their way through the town, many making for the mills.

For most, on this last Thursday of 1888, it would be just another ordinary day. For one local family the day would not be ordinary. Fear would strike, hearts would break, and lives would never be the same.

Mary Ann Gill bustled around her tiny but spotless kitchen humming to herself. She stood in front of the range on the once cheerful rag rug, now much worn out in the middle, waiting for the kettle to boil. While she did so, her family sat around the table chatting as they waited for their tea. The Gills were poor but clean. She lived by her mother's motto from Leviticus 15: "Cleanliness is next to Godliness."

Thomas Gill, husband, father, and local cabman, was proud of his brood of four. He loved his girls, including wee Sammy, but Johnny was his eldest son and there was a strong bond between them.

John, as he was christened, was a handsome, delicate-looking lad with his golden curls and deep, violet-blue eyes. Pretty, almost. He was gentle in nature, thoughtful, friendly, and trusting. Too trusting, some would later say. When people met him for the first time, they noticed him for there was something very special about the lad. He listened with intent when someone spoke and displayed a sharp intellect and maturity far beyond his years. Thomas and Mary Ann Gill tried very hard not to let it show, but Johnny was, without a doubt, their favourite child.

Mary Ann glanced at Thomas as he reached over and playfully ruffled Johnny's hair. The little boy pulled back.

"Aw, Da! Don't do tha'! Mammy's just brushed it!"

"Well lad, you'll be eight soon. You should be brushing your own hair now," Thomas said with a smile.

Thomas was delighted at how the lad was turning out. His teachers at Kirkgate Sunday School consistently sang his praises. Johnny was beginning to show great promise, they said. Tom Gill allowed himself to dream big.

Yes, he thought, *Johnny will be someone one day. Make a name for himself. He won't be a poor cabbie like me. Perhaps he'll be a big manager up at one of them wool mills one day. Perhaps …*

His dreams were rudely interrupted.

The girls, who loved to gang up on their little brother and teased him often, now seized on their father's words.

Ruth, five years older than Johnny, looked over at her younger sister Jane and smiled impishly.

She started chanting, "Johnny is a baby! Johnny is a baby!" Jane needed no encouragement to join in.

Samuel, small as he was, left the table and gave him a protective hug. Johnny hugged his brother in return and carried on pushing his wooden train around the table. Ignoring the girls, he started imitating the noise of the steam trains he saw most days now down at Midland Station with his new friend, Willie Barrett. His mother placed a tin mug of steaming tea in front of him and he quickly discarded the train.

"Ta, Mammy," he said, looking up at her with his big blue eyes, flashing her one of his disarming smiles.

His mother kissed his dimpled cheek while she looked over at the girls in a disapproving manner. She gave them "The Look." They cast their eyes downwards and looked suitably chastised for a fraction of a heartbeat. Then they slyly looked at each other from under their dark eyelashes and started to giggle.

"Johnny, be a good lad an' run up to the stable-yard an' tell George to put a horse in my cab. I'd best be off."

"Okay, Da."

Johnny pushed the train towards Sammy and dashed off, happy for the diversion. In a few minutes, he was back.

"Your horse is in its stall ready for you, Da."

Thomas Gill heaved his frame out of the chair and brushed his lips lightly across the nape of Mary Ann's neck. As he hugged her briefly, he could not help admire how she always managed to keep her hair in a neat and tidy bun, no matter what time of day or what she was doing. One by one, he swung his children around and around as they giggled and squirmed and kissed them all goodbye.

Johnny sat back down at the table and began slurping at his tea impatiently. It was still too hot and he did not want to miss William Barrett's milk cart. He kept jumping up and running to the front window to listen out for it.

"Johnny, will you give over jumping around like a spring cricket on a burning haystack an' come and sup your tea," chided his mother gently. "Willie ain't leaving without you."

"Can I go with our Johnny today, Mammy? Can I? Can I?" asked Samuel, jumping up and down on his short little legs and tugging at his mother's skirts. He had been a couple of times and rather liked going.

She smiled down at him.

"Nay, Sammy. Not today. Today's your wash day. An' besides, you wor to help me peel the oranges for the marmalade, remember?"

Sammy was disappointed. Travelling around with William Barrett on his milk cart was a privilege the children enjoyed. They loved bouncing around in the cart as it travelled over the uneven cobblestones, and enjoyed the responsibility of delivering the milk to his customers. The children were never paid. He took them just for their company, which he seemed to enjoy.

Finally, the rhythmic sound of the horse's iron shoes striking against the flint cobblestones could be heard from some distance away. The sound grew louder as the horse and cart left Manningham Lane and proceeded down the hill towards the house.

Punctuality was ingrained in William Barrett's DNA and he approached the house not a minute later than 7:20.

Before the cart had even time to stop, Johnny had gulped the last of his tea, pushed back his chair and crammed his cap firmly onto his head. He hurriedly kissed his mother goodbye and rushed to open the door. He was halfway across the threshold before she managed to call him back.

"Johnny Gill! You come back this minute an' put your coat on. Are you wanting to cop your death out there?"

"Nay, Mammy," he replied, reluctantly retracing his steps while his mother fussed and fretted as she slipped one arm, and then the other, into his navy-blue topcoat.

"Hurry up, Mam!" he cried impatiently, stamping his little feet to keep warm as she finally did up the last brass button. "We don't want to be late!"

Mary Ann released him as he wriggled out of her grasp to greet Willie Barrett.

"Morning, Willie!" he beamed, before quickly nuzzling up to the brown mare, its vision restricted by the large leather blinkers. Johnny slipped her an apple core that he had saved. She took it lightly from his outstretched palm, the bristles of her muzzle tickling his hand. He giggled.

While Willie waited for Johnny, he lit his pipe, drawing slow and steady on the stem. Then he bent forward and extended a strong hand to the lad, who grabbed it, scrambling into the cart and taking his place beside him. He flicked the reins, urging the horse forward. Johnny looked up at William Barrett, eyes shining with excitement, his smile broad.

As the horse moved and the cart lurched he suddenly remembered his mother. Steadying himself, he clung tightly to the rail and turned to wave goodbye to her as she cried out after them, "Take grand care of the lad for us, Willie!"

Willie Barrett did not turn around. Instead, he lifted his pipe into the air in acknowledgement.

Mary Ann watched as they turned into a hazy outline engulfed by the smog. Then they were gone.

Mr. and Mrs. Cahill walked arm-in-arm along Heaton Road still flushed from the excitement and overindulgence of too much good food and drink from the previous evening. They had been to the annual Servants' Ball at the well-known Alexander Hotel on Great Horton Road.

The Cahills often frequented the Alexander Hotel. They enjoyed its imposing architecture that exuded a genteel grandeur so different from their own humble home. Moreover, they were not the only ones. In the last ten years the hotel had gained an excellent reputation with most of Bradford. It stocked an extensive cellar and the cuisine that it served was legendary. The Alexander had become the best and most well patronized hotel in Bradford under the watchful eye of manager Carlo Fara. Originally from Piedmont, Carlo was now happily ensconced in Bradford, a place he now called home.

The hotel was also well- known as a venue for parties and dances. Dancing at the hotel never started before eleven and the parties usually finished very late. It was because of this that the Cahills had decided to stay over at the Alexander after their Ball. It was also the perfect excuse for a short break away.

On that Wednesday night the Cahills had slept in one of the one hundred and forty rooms the hotel had to offer. They would have loved to have stayed in one of the bigger apartments, but these were way out of their reach. Irrespective of the type of room the couple could afford, they had thoroughly enjoyed their evening at the Alexander, thanks, in no small part, to the accomplished and affable Mr. Fara.

The hotel had become his life. He took pride in being a most congenial manager for whom nothing was too much trouble to ensure pleasing his patrons. Managing it well took up the majority of his time. However, it had not come without some personal cost, for his ignored and neglected wife soon found more willing embraces elsewhere.

Despite this personal setback and his punishing schedule, Carlo was still able to find the time to pursue his interests in the darker sciences of the occult. He had recently become an initiate of the occult group of the Horus Temple, a chapter of the Order of the Golden Dawn recently established in Bradford during the month of October.

Members of the Horus Temple used the Alexander Hotel as a place to gather and hold their meetings. The private apartments were perfect for such an organization and their members now met here regularly every week.

After having had a leisurely breakfast at the hotel, it was just after ten o'clock on the Thursday morning when the Cahills crossed over the tramlines and continued up a gentle incline to their house at number 324 Heaton Road. The house itself was about a half mile from Bradford, and because of its isolated position they had always felt perfectly safe, seldom locking their doors. When they did, the key was always hanging on a nail in a small outhouse close by. Mr. Cahill now walked to the outhouse, took the key off the nail, unlocked the door, and walked inside with Mrs. Cahill trailing behind.

The first thing he noticed, as he entered his house, was an opened umbrella on the floor. It was immediately in front him. He was annoyed as he was not one for actively inviting bad luck. He was about to chastise his wife, but on picking it up and closing, it he realized that it was neither his, nor his wife's.

The front door opened directly into the living room and as they entered it together, Mrs. Cahill screamed. Suspended from their ceiling hung the body of a woman. Her clothes stirred slightly in the stiff breeze from the open door. Once their eyes had adjusted to the light, they realized that it was not a body, but one of his wife's long dresses suspended from a hook in the ceiling, giving only the illusion of a hanging.

A mound of clothing had been unceremoniously dumped on the dining room table, along with a large number of other household items. In addition, on the back of the chair were other items of clothing, but these had been carefully folded with a bonnet placed on top of them.

Looking at her drawing room in disarray with furniture lying upside down and thrown around in some confusion, Mrs. Cahill immediately thought that they had been burgled. However, on looking more closely at the scene in front of them, it became apparent that something far more ominous had taken place.

On a side table were two half-empty glasses. Mr Cahill picked up one of them and smelled the contents. It was, as he suspected, rum. He crossed the room to the kitchen where he kept his stock of rum. A bottle was missing. At this stage, as far as he could tell, this was the only thing missing.

While Mr Cahill was in the kitchen, Mrs. Cahill, too frightened to venture further into her house for fear of someone still being there, hovered in uncertainty. She finally moved around the living room as quietly as she could, all the while wringing her hands in anguish.

On passing the sideboard, she noticed two of her knives crossed over, symbolising a cross and skull bones. Boxes of matches were on their ends, forming a circle around the knives - an additional ritualistic pattern. A large tin can, overfilled with water was next to these; the wood still saturated where it had spilled over.

Placed nearby was a card that was in plain view. Mrs. Cahill picked it up with a trembling hand and read it. On one side of the card was written in pencil, despite pen and ink lying nearby:

'Half-past nine! Look out! Jack the Ripper has been here!'
And on the other side was written,

'I have removed down the canal side. Please drop in!
- Yours truly, SUICIDE.'

She gasped and dropped the card instantly.

By the time Mr. Cahill had moved to the back of the house he had discovered yet another open umbrella. This one was his wife's. He was just bending down to retrieve it when he heard his wife calling him from the next room. She sounded petrified.

"Henry!" she cried. "Come quickly!"

Concerned at the tone of her voice, he came immediately. She pointed to the card that had remained on the floor, her finger trembling, not willing to pick it up again. Mr. Cahill bent down, retrieved the card and read the message.

My God! Was this a prank that someone had played on them? On the other hand, had the Ripper used their isolated house for some disturbing mischief?

He did not know what to think.

Mrs. Cahill broke her husband's gaze as she glanced at the clock on the mantelpiece and inhaled sharply. The clock had been stopped at 9:30, the same time indicated on the card. She was well acquainted with the custom of stopping a clock at the hour of death. However, whose death did it indicate? Hers? Her husband's?

"Henry, please search the house to see if someone is still here."

She paced the room while Mr. Cahill moved quietly throughout the rest of the house looking for the intruders.

After a short while, he was by her side again.

"They've gone, my dear," he said gently. "There is no one here."

Despite his reassurance, Mrs. Cahill was not placated.

"We need to fetch a constable at once, Henry! No one knew that we would be at the hotel last night except your employer. No one! I'm terrified, Henry! Jack the Ripper was here? In our house? This whole situation is terrifying!

"And while you're out looking for a constable I shall be packing our things. Because I'm telling you now, Henry Cahill, when we leave here today I am *never* setting foot in this house again!"

Mary Ann Gill bent over the cast iron pot with its bubbling contents of glistening, golden marmalade. It plopped and hissed as the steam escaped and she tamed it with a wooden spoon for a while, stirring it down.

She kept glancing at the clock on the opposite wall in the front room. Johnny was late. It was not like him at all. It was already 11:25 and he was always home by eleven. She was annoyed at his tardiness. She removed the marmalade from the fire and allowed it to cool slightly before pouring it carefully into the sterilized jars she had neatly lined up on the table.

After thirty more long minutes had passed her exasperation and annoyance was now morphing into anxiety. She wrung her hands on her apron several times and kept opening the door and looking up and down the road.

It is not like the lad at all, she thought.

She closed the door for the umpteenth time and moved to the window. Turgid clouds that had threatened rain all day had finally released a deluge onto the grimy town, scrubbing Bradford clean. She watched as the rain struck and bounced off the cobbles, forming pools where poorly constructed drains were beginning to block up in protest. She did not like to think that Johnny was out there in this weather getting soaked.

Thirty more minutes passed and now she was very apprehensive.

"Where could the lad be? He's over an hour late! Where could he be?" she asked aloud in a strained voice. She was seeking reassurance from her daughters, who were in the room with her. However, both were too self-absorbed and preoccupied to care. Mary Ann nervously pulled on a dark strand of hair that had escaped from her usually neat bun and continued pacing the room.

Thirteen-year-old Ruth, who had been up early and had already worked several hours at Holden's Mill, was tired. She did not share her mother's anxiety. She was just pleased to be home and to be able to spend time with her sister. She liked the Christmas holidays. For a few days of the year, she did not have to attend the schoolroom after a shift at the noisy mill.

Mary Ann looked at Ruth sprawled out on the front room floor attempting to draw her kitten, which was not being a cooperative subject. Jane was equally busy. The ever-changing colours that appeared in her new kaleidoscope, at every turn, captivated her. They were both far too busy with their Christmas presents to be worried about their little brother, whom they were sure would come bursting through the door at any moment.

It was only when Ruth glanced up momentarily that she saw the anxiety etched on her mother's face. It took her by surprise.

"Don't fret, Ma, he'll be home soon," she said reassuringly. She watched her mother wearing out a path from the kitchen to the front window, the same window that Johnny had used hours earlier looking out for Willie Barrett.

The tiny panes of sash window that limited her vision frustrated Mary Ann. She opened the door once again and stepped out into the cold, looking up and down the road. She hugged her arms and rubbed them through her thin, cotton dress as she turned right, looking towards the busy thoroughfare of Manningham Lane. There was no sign of him. She turned to her left, hoping to see him coming up the road from the direction of Barrett's house in Bateman Street. He was not there either. She reluctantly stepped back inside her house and closed the door.

"Ruth, leave what you're doing. Go up to the dairy an' see if you can find your brother. An' take Jane with you. Perhaps Johnny is helping Mr. Barrett an' the lads up there with summat. An' if he's there, bring him home straight away, will you? An' you can tell him from me when you see him that I'm right cross with him. He's going to get a right walloping!"

The Ashfield Dairy was only one hundred and fifty yards away in Manningham Lane and so it was not long before the girls returned.

"Well? Where's your brother then?" demanded Mary Ann, standing in the kitchen with her hands on her hips.

"No idea, Mammy. We went up to the dairy, but Mr. Barrett worn't there. He wor out delivering milk. P'rhaps our John is playing with friends. Shall I knock on some doors and see where he is, then?"

"There's a good lass. Would you mind?"

The girls knocked on countless doors in the neighbourhood, but the answer was always the same. He was not there. No one had seen him.

Two more hours went by before Mary Ann said, "Ruth, take care of your sister and Samuel, an' stay here. I'm going to nip on down to Mrs. Barrett's to see if he's there."

She grabbed her shawl and stepped outside, not bothering to remove her apron. Nor did she notice that although the rain had stopped, deep puddles of water were everywhere. She forged through them oblivious that the last four inches of her faded calico skirt and petticoats were now soaking wet and laced with mud.

Within minutes, Mary Ann had reached Barrett's back-to-back house. She lifted the latch to the wrought iron gate and closed it carefully behind her. The uneven steps along the ascending path to the three-storey house bordered a small patch of unkempt garden. She took no notice of the dying flowers and flourishing weeds.

She knocked rapidly on the door and then stepped back onto the tread below. While she waited, she focused on the door. It was shedding its paint like a blue lizard in the process of ecdysis. She shifted her feet and played nervously with the loose strands of hair around her face. She was not even sure if this was the right house. Although William Barrett had been doing the milk run for more than a month now, the family had only moved into the neighbourhood a week before Christmas.

She strained her ears but could hear nothing. Then she heard a baby wailing in the background. After what seemed like an eternity, the door finally opened. Young Mrs. Barrett stood on the threshold with baby Nellie in her arms, her squalling quelled with the help of a rattle hurriedly placed in her small, tight fist.

Margaret Barrett looked at the woman in front of her. She seemed vaguely familiar but she could not quite place her.

"I'm Johnny Gill's mother. Your husband takes my lad on his milk cart sometimes."

"Oh, Mrs. Gill!" She smiled, finally recognising who she was. "Aye?"

"Well, Mr. Barrett took our Johnny on his round this morning an' he should've been back hours ago, but he hasn't come home. I'm dead worried about him. I wor wondering if he'd come back with him an' wor here."

"Nay. The lad wor here this morning when Willie come for his breakfast. Willie wor here again just now at twelve but he come on his own. He said nowt about your Johnny. If I see him, I'll tell him you wor looking for him."

Mary Ann thanked the woman and hurried back up the hill. Her anxiety was rapidly becoming full-blown fear. Her heart was racing and her hands were clammy, despite the weather. She was fighting hard to keep her emotions under control. She was so preoccupied with her anxious thoughts that she passed her best friend on the street without even realizing she had done so.

"Mary Ann! It's me! You just passed me by! All right, are you?"

Annie Kershaw looked at her friend's unusual pallor and unfocused eyes.

"Ee bah Gum, Mary Ann! What's happened?"

When she repeated her question, she did so in earnest, as Mary Ann still had made no response. She shook her friend's arm gently.

Mary Ann came out of her fog of fear and uncertainty and slowly focused on the woman who appeared in front of her. She stared at the mouth that was talking, but heard no sound. Recognition finally kicked in. She clutched Annie's arm in gratitude.

"Oh! Annie! It's you! Wee Johnny went off with Willie Barrett this morning but he hasn't come home. I'm dead worried summat has happened to him." Her voice quivered as she spoke, but somehow she managed to hold on to the tears that were threatening to spill over.

"Nay, Mary Ann. Give over your fretting. He's probably larking around with some lads an' has forgotten the time. You know what lads are like. Did you nip on down to Bateman Street?"

"Aye, I did. I've just come from there. Mrs. Barrett ain't seen him since this morning. It's right strange. After the round, Johnny always comes straight home. Always! He knows he ain't allowed to play in the streets until he's told me. I'm right worried, Annie, I am." And with that, the welling tears she had been battling to hold onto spilled over and coursed down her plump cheeks.

"Hush now, Mary Ann. Don't fret," Annie said, linking her arm through Mary Ann's and patting her hand reassuringly. "Let's nip on up the street an' see where he is, shall we?"

They continued up the road to the busy thoroughfare of Manningham Lane, making inquiries of shopkeepers, friends, and neighbours they saw in the street. They even resorted to accosting perfect strangers. All the while, Annie was trying desperately to allay her friend's growing fears.

After scouring the streets and lanes of the neighbourhood for over two hours, both women returned home exhausted and concerned. They turned into Thorncliffe Road and walked the short distance down the hill towards the house. Mary Ann passed her front-room window with the copper downpipe clinging precariously to the stonework, walked up the short flagged path, and pushed open the door. She fervently hoped that Johnny would be waiting for her. He was not.

At about three o' clock, there was a knock at the door and Annie went to see who it was. It was William Barrett.

Mary Ann rushed to the door when she heard his voice, hope surging that he would tell her where her Johnny was.

'Willie! Do you know where Johnny is?"

"Johnny hasn't come home?

"Nay. Ain't he with you?

Her heart sank in deepening distress as she listened to him speak while he stood there turning his billycock hat repeatedly in his hands.

"Nay. Johnny left me at Walmer Villas at about eight-thirty this morning. He said he wor going home for breakfast. The last time I saw him he wor sliding down some icy patches in the street, larking about with some lads."

The news was unexpected. Her breath shortened. Her heart raced as she listened to him relating the last whereabouts of Johnny's movements. Her thoughts were slow, as if they were moving through treacle. She tried to process them, but fear and anxiety swamped her mind, leaving it bereft of reason. Questions that should have been asked were not. Barrett took his leave.

Mary Ann's hand trembled as she placed it on the cold brass knob and shut the door. She now knew that Johnny had been missing since early this morning. She felt sick. Leaning forward with her forehead on the back of the door she shut her eyes and prayed as she had never prayed before.

Please God, make sure nothing has happened to our Johnny an' bring him home safe to us. Please God! Please make sure he is safe!

She continued to pray fervently. Begging. Bargaining. Pleading for her boy's safe return. God did not reply.

Annie and Mary Ann sat in the kitchen trying to make sense of it all.

"Annie, where could he be? It ain't like him. Johnny never just goes off on his own like this."

"It's right strange. But perhaps he had his reasons."

"Aye. But why? Perhaps Willie said summat to upset him. I can't think why he would've just left him like that."

"Walmer Villas isn't that far away. He can't have gone too far."

"I am sure too that Walmer Villas is the last place Willie delivers milk, before he goes back to the dairy. Why would our Johnny have left him to walk home when he could've come back with the cart five minutes later? It doesn't make any sense."

As they continued to speak Mary Ann's thoughts started to crystallize, and she found Barrett's explanation lacking and rather odd. The more and more she thought about it, the more she felt that she needed to tell him that.

Leaving the girls at home with Annie, she walked the short distance to the dairy in search of the man. She had no difficulty finding him this time. He was scrubbing out his milk cans for the evening delivery.

She had to stand and wait for him to finish his conversation with Mr. Wolfenden, his employer and owner of the popular Ashfield Dairy. She overheard them discussing a lost key. She waited quietly, her hand involuntarily reaching out for her hair once again and twisting a strand unconsciously.

"Willie, what about that key missing from the stables? No sign of it then, I take it?"

"Nay, I haven't seen it. Mind you, it's only been a week. Hopefully, it'll turn up soon."

Suddenly the men were aware that they were not alone, and they acknowledged Mary Ann's presence. Wolfenden went back to his office and she lost no time in telling Barrett why she had come. After Wolfenden had left, Barrett had gone back to cleaning his milk cans. He continued to scrub them as she spoke.

"Willie, how many places had you to deliver milk at when our Johnny left you?"

"One," was the short response.

Her question had caused him to look up briefly. He now remained bent over the churns, the scrubbing brush in his right hand, his elbow resting on the rim and his left arm taking his weight. He offered up no more and then went back to his scrubbing.

"Tell me, Willie, why would he have done that? Why would he have left you one stop before the round was up? He's never done that before. An' besides, you would've passed him going back to the depot. He'd only have been two minutes away from the end of the round. He could've come back with you on the cart - like he always does. What happens to a child over such a short distance of two hundred yards that he doesn't make it home? It doesn't make any sense." Her voice quavered as she asked him but she still managed to remain calm, waiting for his reply.

William Barrett looked up briefly and shrugged, seemingly unmoved by her distress.

"I didn't pass him."

She waited, willing him to say more, but as a man of few words he did not, and continued scrubbing out the cans. It was pointless to stay.

The hours of waiting for Johnny to appear had not only taken their toll, but a profound feeling of impending doom had engulfed her. The feeling was invading every synapse of her system with every step that she took towards home. Feelings of hope were now being edged out. Despair was taking its place. When she returned she collapsed into a nearby chair. Annie looked at her expectantly, waiting to hear some news, but Mary Ann struggled to convey her feelings of just how she felt and started to sob instead.

Alarmed by their mother's distress the girls came running from their room. For the first time they realized that perhaps something might well have happened to their little brother. They flung themselves onto their mother and they too started to cry.

Annie rushed over. She dropped to her knees and wrapped her arms around them all, comforting them as best she could.

"Summat dreadful has happened to our Johnny, Annie. I just know it," Mary Ann finally managed to get out in between the sobs.

She continued to cry deep, guttural sobs as Annie tried to comfort her as best she could with platitudes, empty platitudes that people say at times like these. Some say them because they cannot find the words to express what they feel. There are others, where the incomprehensibility of agreeing is too dreadful to contemplate. It was the latter with which Annie was struggling.

"Now, now, Mary Ann. Don't fret. We'll find him. I promise," she said, placing a comforting hand on her back and patting it from time to time.

Five-year-old Samuel, awoken from his nap with his mother's weeping, was confused at the unfamiliar noise around him and he too started to cry. Annie got up off the floor, bent down, scooped him up, and cuddled him. She placed him on her broad hip and jiggled him up and down to stop him from crying. Once he had stopped, she turned to Ruth.

"Come now, Ruth, dry your tears. We can't cry over summat that hasn't happened. Run along with Jane an' see if you can find your Da an' tell him to come and see your Mam. She needs him to find out where your Johnny is. Don't tarry too long," she said brusquely.

She placed Samuel down, gently prised the girls away from their distressed mother, and bundled them into their coats and hats. The girls dried their eyes and noses with the backs of their sleeves. They were still sniffing when they went in search of their father.

Annie reached into her warm, ample bosom for her clean hankie and pressed it into Mary Ann's hand.

Samuel's tears dried up as soon as she gave him a biscuit. With him settled, she proceeded to brew a strong cup of tea for the both of them. Because, truth be told, she did not know what else to do.

******

Ruth and Jane finally found Thomas on Lumb Lane, just as he was dropping off one of his regular passengers. He pulled the horse up short when he saw his girls racing towards him, petticoats flying and shouting his name repeatedly. Tom immediately jumped down from the cab and was alarmed at the sight of them. As they drew nearer he could see that their faces were stained with tears and their eyes were red.

"Whoa, slow down! What's wrong?"

It took him a while before he could get any sense out of them. For as soon as they had seen him both the girls had simultaneously flung their arms around his thickening waist and had broken out in a fresh round of tears. He felt awkward as he stood there on the busy street pacifying the two weeping girls as strangers walked slowly by and stared.

Eventually, between the sobs and talking in unison, they explained why they had come to fetch him. Thomas was a practical man, and he could think of dozens of acceptable reasons as to why the lad wasn't home yet. Several possibilities of why he could be late flitted through his mind without even thinking too hard.

Perhaps he had been playing with friends and they had found a diversion in going fishing up at Bradford Beck. Or maybe he had gone up to the market to buy a bag of humbugs and had stopped to help one of the men with their stalls. He may have even gone further afield to Leonard Robinson's shop in Manchester Road in search of his famous brandy snaps.

Johnny was a sensible lad and had been given some money for Christmas. Tom remembered that he intended to save most of it and was looking forward to putting it aside in the bank after the holidays. However, he hadn't wanted to save all of it. Possibly then, he had gone off to buy something special with his money and had forgotten the time.

Tom was sure that there was a perfectly good explanation for his son's absence. With this in mind he lifted the girls into the carriage, turned into Grosvenor Street, and headed for home. He would seek out Mary Ann and find out exactly what all the fuss was about.

It wasn't until he arrived back at the house that his confidence about where his boy could be was shattered. He was appalled by Mary Ann's account of Willie Barrett's story. He swiftly shared his wife's concern.

He too thought the story of Johnny leaving the round so close to home mighty peculiar and decided that it was time to take the cab and scour the streets himself. He needed to start asking questions and getting some answers. He would start with Willie Barrett.

Barrett could not be found. Thomas realized, not too long into his journey, that there were more questions than answers. He had spoken to several people in the vicinity where Johnny had last been seen. And according to some,

Johnny was still with Barrett long after he had told Mary Ann that the lad had left him. Nothing was adding up.

He returned home more worried than when he had set out. He tried to comfort Mary Ann as best he could, who was now beside herself with worry. And their patience was being tested when neighbours, who had heard the news that one of their own had gone missing, began stopping by at number 41 Thorncliffe Road.

Some neighbours were genuine in their concern and offered to help look for the lad, for which they were grateful. Others, many of whom the Gills had never seen before, were there for the excitement and to feed off gossip. As others drifted in Annie Kershaw decided to take her leave to see to her own grown-up family that had been sorely neglected by the day's events. When she left she took the two girls and Samuel with her to give Mary Ann and Thomas some respite.

For Mary Ann and Thomas everything was a blur. They desperately wanted to be alone, to be able to talk openly to one another and to find out what the other knew. However, with a house full of people, each offering their opinion on the matter, they were finding it exceedingly difficult. The gossipmongers that crowded their front room were hovering like extras in a play. Their presence was suffocating, their opinions toxic.

Thomas decided that he would take the initiative. As politely as he could he thanked everyone for coming and hoped they understood if he and his wife needed to be on their own. The large gathering eventually dispersed and Mary Ann and Thomas were finally able to talk.

"Did you find out anything, Tom?" asked Mary Ann as soon as the last person had left. She was holding both his hands up against her chest in a tight grip, pleading with her eyes as she searched his face, hoping for a flicker of hope, an inkling of something positive. However, his eyes reflected not the assurance she was looking for. Instead, they reflected feelings of despondency and trepidation.

"What wor folk saying? Where is our Johnny? He can't just have disappeared into thin air! He has to be somewhere!"

"I agree with you, Mary Ann. I tried to find Barrett to ask him what had happened to Johnny, but I couldn't find him. He should know where Johnny is, of all folk."

"Aye, but that's the strange thing, he doesn't. He wor here several times today asking about Johnny. He came by again at eight this evening while you wor out an' asked the same question. I just don't understand why our Johnny would've left him so soon before the round. I keep asking him if he said summat to the lad that would've caused him to leave so unexpectedly an' he said that he hadn't. I've told him twice now; odd it is that the lad left when he did, so soon before the end of the round. But he says nowt. He just stands there, turning his hat round an' round, an' gazes down the road. I want to shake him to get summat, anything out of him. But he just stands there an' says nowt!"

Mary Ann became increasingly agitated as she spoke. Sobs followed the outbreak.

For once in his life, Tom Gill felt adrift like a weightless barque tossed upon a stormy sea. He was trying to piece together what little he knew so far and he was frustrated by the fact that nothing seemed to fit. For the first time he allowed himself to wonder if something sinister had happened to his lad. His thoughts were dark. He dispelled them as quickly as they had come.

Later that night, together with some friends, Thomas Gill searched the streets of Manningham and this time, far beyond. He spoke to residents, scoured the now empty markets, the station, the infirmary. Tom even went back to the dairy. He went to every place where he thought Johnny might have been. He searched the town centre to see if he could find him there. He even went out to the coal pits and to the quarry between St. Mark's Church and Manningham Lane. He repeatedly called Johnny's name in case he had fallen into a shaft or down a hole at the quarry. However, he was nowhere to be found. It was indeed as if he had just vanished into thin air.

Copious mugs of tea later, in the small hours of the morning with sleep eluding both of them, Mary Ann and Thomas finally came to a decision. They would take Tom's patient horse that was still tied to the copper downpipe, forgotten about in the extraordinary circumstances, and go to Town Hall to make a missing person's report with the constable on duty. Mary Ann also wanted to put an advertisement in the local newspaper of Johnny's disappearance in the hope that someone reading it might have seen something and would bring it to the attention of the police.

At 4:00 a.m., Thomas and Mary Ann Gill took his cab and proceeded to Town Hall. As Thomas flicked the reins from time to time and steered the horse towards their destination, he did so with a heavy heart. Making a missing person's report was an official admission that Johnny was missing and not just late in coming home. Too many hours had passed for him to be just larking about with friends.

The possibility that something dark had now taken root, was weighing heavily on his mind.

CHAPTER TWO - FRIDAY 28ᵀᴴ DECEMBER 1888

Friday would be a very strange day indeed for many Bradford residents. Some things would appear significant after the event, while other events would prove to be quite bizarre at the time.

Thomas sat with Mary Ann in the kitchen utterly exhausted. Each was engrossed in their thoughts, not willing to say what the other was thinking. It was just before 7:00 a.m. They had spent half the night and the small hours of the morning trawling the streets with many willing neighbours trying to find their boy, but to no avail. They were emotionally battered and bruised.

When they saw the advertisement that they had placed in the local newspaper just hours before, Mary Ann started to weep again and Thomas kept swallowing hard.

'Lost on Thursday morning a boy, John Gill, aged 8. Was last seen in Walmer-villas at 8:30 a.m. Had on navy-blue top-coat (with brass buttons on), midshipman's cap, plaid Knickerbocker suit, laced boots, red and black stockings. Complexion fair; home, 41 Thorncliffe-road.'

Tom got up abruptly and put on his coat and cap. He was angry. He was angry at Barrett for allowing the lad to wander off like that. He was angry at himself for not being there to protect his family better. He was angry at his inability to find his son. He took his brooding thoughts with him and began searching for his boy once more. He was exhausted, but he felt useless just sitting around waiting. Thomas was determined to bring his boy home safely and he wasn't going to do that sitting at the kitchen table drinking mugs of tea.

Mary Ann had an agenda of her own. She was desperate to talk to Barrett again. She was hoping that by this morning he had remembered something. She needed to see him, to talk to him. In some strange way, Mary Ann felt drawn to him. He was the link to her Johnny. He was the last person to have seen her lad. She felt that if she just asked the right questions, perhaps he would remember something that would unlock the mystery of his disappearance.

But Barrett was not about and she was frustrated by the fact. It wasn't until just before noon that there was another knock at the door. William Barrett was standing outside her house looking awkward, billycock in hand.

"Has Johnny come?" he asked, as he had done several times now over the last two days.

"Nay, he hasn't," replied an increasingly fraught Mary Ann. "We've been seeking all over for the lad, all through the night. We haven't found him anywhere. Willie, what can you tell me? Where's our Johnny?"

William Barrett cast his eyes to the ground and left without uttering a response. Not a single word.

The hours passed and grey shadows grew longer. People came and went; faceless voices expressing the same concerns, the same opinions, the same platitudes. The one thing that she and Tom wanted no one could provide. Who had seen their lad and where was he?

It was well-nigh ten that night and she still hadn't heard from, or seen Barrett since midday. His lack of response to her questions was eating away at her insides like rampant cancer. Finally, she decided that Barrett would have to be home by now and he would have to tell her something.

She made the familiar trip down to Bateman Street, passing 24 Cliffe Terrace, where she fetched her children from Annie Kershaw and took her along for moral and emotional support. Once again she knocked on the peeling door, but despite the late hour, Barrett was not at home. The small group, feeling dejected, made their way slowly up the hill. They had just reached Thorn Terrace when they encountered Barrett walking towards them on his way home.

"Willie, I've come to ask you, beg you to tell me what's happened to our lad. You have to say summat, please! I feel sick with worry! Did you say summat cross to Johnny? Put me out of my misery an' tell me where he is. Can you tell me anything?" She made her plea through a stream of tears. With each additional question her voice was becoming more strident.

Annie could see that Mary Ann was quite distraught. She placed a comforting arm around her while the children, surrounded by their own feelings of confusion, clung to the women's skirts and wept. Annie was beginning to feel overwhelmed by the enormity of the situation that she had found herself part of. She loved the little lad like one of her own. She felt keenly for Mary Ann.

Barrett replied with his usual monosyllabic response, "Nay."

He turned to go, but Mary Ann blocked his path.

"Well, you'll have to know summat soon! The detectives are coming up in the morning for you, Willie Barrett. An' then you'll have to tell them summat."

"All right," he replied. And with that he continued down the road.

Mary Ann and Annie looked at one another. Words were left unspoken. They kissed and hugged as they got to the corner of Thorncliffe Road and Cliffe Terrace, said goodbye, and returned to their respective houses.

A steady stream of folk from far and wide continued to arrive at the Gills; many for the vicarious thrill of being part of an unfolding and deepening mystery. With each passing hour, with still no news on where her child could be, Mary Ann was finding it tedious repeating the story to so many, over and over again. The strain was beginning to show.

Perhaps it was someone's kindness, or something someone said, or a culmination of all that had gone before, but without warning, out of the blue, the realization struck her. There was a strong possibility that Johnny was never coming back. She gasped in pain as the weight of the knowledge crushed her chest. Doubling up in her chair she rocked back and forth, a mournful sound emanating from deep within. Startled by her display of distress, those that were there departed in haste and finally left her in peace.

No sooner had the last visitor left when there was another knock at the door. Tom's heart jumped. Every time there was a knock he hoped that it would be someone telling him that they had found his lad. He left comforting Mary Ann to answer it.

He tried to hide his disappointment when he saw it was only Annie. Despite the late hour she was holding on to a steaming pot of soup and dumplings that somehow, between looking after her family and comforting Mary Ann, she had found the time to make.

She didn't wait for an invitation to step across the threshold. As a good friend and neighbour such niceties in situations like these were wholly unnecessary. Instead, she sailed in and made herself at home in the kitchen. She fetched a collection of mismatching bowls down from the dresser, rummaged around for some spoons in the drawer and started ladling out the soup.

"That's right kind of you, Annie," said Tom politely. He wasn't hungry but he couldn't remember when last he ate, nor was he even sure when the children had last eaten. Suddenly, he was very grateful for people like Annie Kershaw.

"Nonsense, Tom!" she replied, "That's what friends are for."

After they had eaten their soup, Annie put the children to bed and heard their prayers to bring Johnny back safely. When she returned she found Tom and Mary Ann looking utterly disconsolate. Mary Ann's eyes were red from a combination of relentless crying and lack of sleep. Her bowl of soup remained untouched. Her anguish was palpable.

"Try an' get some sleep," she said kindly. "I'll stay up an' wait here for news of Johnny.

Tom was grateful for her offer but he wanted to be there when Johnny came back to find out where he had been. He wanted to be there so that he could wrap his arms around him and to tell him how much he loved him. Sitting around waiting; waiting for news, waiting for something, anything, made him feel helpless. Helplessness was a strange feeling that did not sit well.

Finally, exhaustion was taking hold. No matter how much he had been trying to fight it off, trying desperately to keep awake, he wasn't winning the battle. And neither was Mary Ann. She was still sitting at the table, hearing but not listening while Annie Kershaw made small talk, still trying to be positive.

Annie reiterated what she had said earlier. "Try an' get some sleep both of you an' don't worry," she reassured them, "I'll stay up an' call you as soon as I hear summat."

Mary Ann smiled weakly at her friend to convey her thanks as Tom led her by the hand as they made their way to their tiny bedroom on the top floor.

As Tom lay in the dark he wondered how much sleep he would get. He fervently hoped that when he woke up the last two day's events would prove to be just a horrible nightmare. He prayed too that life would return to normal and his family, once again, would be together and complete.

******

Police Constable Arthur Kirk had drawn the short straw for night patrol that Friday. Sleep for him would not be an option. Despite the plummeting temperatures, brought on by a cloudless sky, he would be tramping the streets of Manningham keeping its residents safe. When he started his Thorncliffe Road beat at 9:00 p.m. that night he knew that he wouldn't finish until six the following morning.

It was going to be a long night, not helped by his footwear. His new boots were damp and two sizes too big. Last night they had chafed the backs of his heels and given him blisters. Ill-fitting boots were not what one needed for a job where one had to be on one's feet, but Arthur Kirk was a diligent man who took his job rather seriously. Despite the discomfort he walked the beat several times that night, each time writing in his little book the times he had made security checks on the various buildings that fell under his protection.

One of the buildings on his beat was a stable and coach house belonging to Mr. Berwick, the butcher. The building was in Back Mellor Street, just off Thorncliffe Road. Buildings along this obscure thoroughfare were used mainly as storehouses by tradesmen and visited infrequently. The exception was Berwick's stable, which was used daily.

Despite the presence of gaslamps, certain recesses along this lane were so deep that no gaslight could reach them. And the presence of uneven stones in the paving made it dangerous to walk this area without the aid of a Bullseye lamp. The only area along the lane that was well-lit came from a house that backed onto the thoroughfare. Here a light burned all night. The occupants were an elderly man and his son, the former having an on-going and protracted illness that caused him to get up several times during the night.

Arthur Kirk approached the stables and coach house belonging to Mr. Berwick and tried the handle for the first time at 10:25 p.m. It was locked. He shone his Bullseye oil lamp in and around the recesses of the immediate area and up and down the coach house and stables. All was clear. He took out the stubby pencil from behind his ear and noted his findings in his little black book.

As a policeman on the beat his job was to cover two and a half miles, every hour. His point of return to the stables was almost at regular two-hour intervals. At 12:25 a.m., 2:25 a.m. and 4:35 a.m. P. C. Kirk tried the doors to Berwick's Stables and found them locked. He shone the lamp into all the dark corners of the thoroughfare and each time noted his findings.

As the light grew broader and the stars grew faint it had been an uneventful shift. The type of shift Arthur Kirk looked forward to.

Old man Dodsworth and his son lived in Mellor Street, opposite the same stables that Constable Kirk had searched on his beat on Friday night. It was his house that had the all-night light that made Arthur Kirk's job a lot easier.

Being an invalid now he didn't sleep very well at the best of times. On Friday night, he was particularly poorly. Although he had gone to bed just after 11:15 he had needed to use the toilet several times before daybreak. But despite a broken night's sleep, he had not seen anything, nor heard anything, that would have aroused suspicion.

Benjamin Abbot, a local draper at 125 Manningham Lane, was sewing the last hem to the yellow chintz curtains. It was 10:30 p.m. and it had been a long day. He snipped the final thread and felt content. He had finally finished the large order for the wealthy German wool trader's wife well before time. If he continued in this vein he would soon have enough money to expand his business and move closer to town. The prospect pleased him.

He carefully placed each set of curtains into pale lilac striped boxes, replaced the lids, and stacked them for delivery first thing in the morning. Feeling very satisfied, he closed the door and locked up for the night. It was just before 10:45 p.m.

He made his way to his house on Lumb Lane, via Back Belle Vue, as he did every night. And suddenly, there it was again. A light was coming from the top window of the stable opposite the Servants' Home. And he made a mental note of it. For this was the second time, within so many days, that he had seen the light coming from the stables at such an unusual time of night. In all the years that he had owned the drapers shop and had walked home the same route every night, he had never seen light coming from there before, at that particular hour.

Richard Manuel, a butcher by trade, was in high spirits. He had taken part in the billiard handicap at the Conservative Club on Manningham Lane that evening. The night had been an excellent one but unfortunately, Richard had stayed out longer than anticipated. It was already 11:45 p.m. and he knew that if he did not make it home soon his nagging wife would be having plenty to say. He picked up the pace so that he would be home before midnight in order to keep the peace.

He walked past the Wolfenden stables at 11 Back Belle Vue and saw a light coming from the top window. On approaching closer he noticed that a man was holding the stable door open with his left hand. He passed close enough to see that he was wearing a dark all-in-one coat and a pair of cotton worsted trousers. However, the man did not attempt to conceal his presence and suspicion at the time was not raised.

Richard Manuel, more worried about seeing his wife at his front door, rather than seeing a stranger at his, thought nothing more of it and continued on his way.

Eliza Jane Kendall, widow and matron of the Bell Vue Servants' House, suddenly sat bolt upright in her bed.

She had been startled by a strange noise coming in the direction of the stables. Her back room faced the stable-yard; it was almost opposite the entrance gates and her window was open by about four inches. She wasn't sure of the time, but she knew that it was somewhere between one and three o'clock in the morning. She often heard manure being scrapped up off the floor during the early morning hours while she was still lying in bed. But it was too early for that. This was an entirely different sound.

Her heart was pounding. She could feel it reverberating and echoing inside her throat. At first she had wondered if a burglar was trying to break into the house. She held her breath. She listened carefully, trying to ignore the pounding of her beating heart. But the more she listened, the more she realized that the noise was not coming from the house. It was definitely coming from the stable. It was a sound like nothing she had ever heard. She was having trouble identifying it.

It sounded like someone was rubbing something, a friction noise, backwards and forwards, backwards and forwards. Swish, swish, swish, swish. At times it became a little louder. She sat up in bed straining her ears trying to make out what it was. Was it scraping, swilling, scrubbing, sawing? She couldn't tell. For ten or twelve minutes the noise continued. Eventually, it stopped. She started to breathe more easily.

Was that a door shutting? She wasn't sure. But she clearly heard hurried footsteps moving away from the stables. They were going in the direction of Manningham Lane.

She lay back on her pillow and listened for a minute or two longer. On hearing nothing more she turned onto her side and tried to get back to sleep.

CHAPTER THREE - SATURDAY 29TH DECEMBER 1888

For the Gill family, Thursday had blurred into Friday, which had blurred into Saturday, with little differentiation in between. Sleep, which would have naturally divided the days, had eluded them both.

Young Theresa Lindley worked a morning shift up at Holden's Mill, and this Saturday morning was no different. She lived at 19 Bateman Street, neighbour to William and Margaret Bateman, who had recently moved in at number 24.

The knocker-up had come by at 5:00 a.m. and thirty minutes later, she knew she needed to get a jiggle on if she did not want to be late. With no one else up in the household yet, she let herself out as quietly as she could and stepped out onto the doorstep, into the cold and dark.

It was not that dark that she could not see William Barrett coming down his front path. Theresa watched him close the wrought-iron gate behind him and turn onto the street, walking slightly ahead of her. As far as she knew, he always started his day at least an hour later. His movements piqued her, as she had never seen him up so early before.

He continued up the road and turned into Thorncliffe Road. She followed, walking on the opposite side. When they had reached Manningham Lane, Theresa turned left at the T-junction towards Holden's Mill. She looked back over her shoulder to see where Barrett had gone. By this time, he had crossed over to the other side of the road and was turning right into Belle Vue, home of Wolfenden's Stables.

She carried on walking towards the mill, past the park, and then up Apsley Crescent, all the while thinking that in light of the missing child that was last seen in his company, his actions were rather unusual.

Young Lizzie Jefferson was a servant at the Servants' Home and had been busy doing her chores for the day. Her day started at 5:30 a.m., and thirty minutes later, she needed to go into the scullery that overlooked Wolfenden's Stables.

As she entered the scullery for the third time that morning, she noticed that light was coming from the stable, and she could hear someone whistling and then hammering at something. She must be late. She checked the hallway clock to make sure. She was surprised to see that it had just gone six o'clock. The stable was never opened much before 7:00 a.m.

She used to set her watch by it.

John Thomas Dyer was not particularly bright. Put under pressure he was easily confused as to whether his name was John Thomas, or Thomas John. Nevertheless, despite his intellectual shortcomings he was a pleasant enough lad, and perfectly harmless. He loved people and enjoyed striking up conversations with them on his way to and from work. He was rather proud of his part-time employment as a boot shiner for Major Churchill up at the big house. However, people being people, they often dismissed young John Thomas for the simpleton he was and hurried on their way.

However, someone who had given him the time of day was William Barrett. Therefore, when he saw Barrett come out of a back gate next to the Wolfenden stables at 6:20 that morning carrying a heavy and cumbersome bundle in front of him, John Thomas was quick to recognize him. He attempted to talk to him, as he usually did.

"Good morning, sir. Bless the Lord! Hallelujah!" He finished the salutation with his customary salute.

Today Barrett did not return the greeting. Instead, he bent his head, avoided eye contact and kept his eyes on the ground. Dyer was disappointed. Barrett had never ignored him before. However, because people often avoided him, instead of walking abreast with Barrett, as he would have done had he greeted him, he now walked several paces behind.

Although Dyer could not keep up with Barrett, he did see him cross over Manningham Lane, go down into Thorncliffe Road, and walk in the direction of Mellor Street.

A young woman, stranger to these parts, lived at Bolton Woods near Frizinghall just outside of Bradford. She had stayed overnight with friends who lived on Thornton Road. Although she would have liked to stay a little longer, she needed to get back home early that morning to sort out some personal affairs. Therefore, it came about that she was out on the streets, earlier than most.

As she was walking along Manningham Lane at about 6:30 a.m. going in the direction of Thorncliffe Road, she happened to notice a man walking in front of her. He was struggling with something heavy. Whatever he was transporting, he was carrying it rather carefully.

As she walked towards him, she almost drew parallel to him when he turned down into Thorncliffe Road. As he turned, she noticed that he was carrying a bundle of clothes on top of two outstretched arms. As she was walking further along Manningham Lane she saw that he was now just below a butcher's shop, about twelve yards from Mellor Street. That was the last she saw of him.

She did not see his features nor did she know who he was. However, she did notice that he wore a dark coat and a billycock and that his shoulders were broad. However, this impression might have been due to the way he was carrying the bundle. However, there was just something about him that made her take particular notice.

Thomas Gill had not slept much since Thursday night. He was utterly exhausted. He sat at the kitchen table drinking a mug of tea. His eyes were bloodshot and sore. He placed the enamel mug back on the table and rubbed his eyelids with his index fingers. His thumbs rested on his cheeks and he could feel a two-day stubble of an unshaven face beneath them. He glanced at the clock - it was just after 6:30 a.m.

While gazing ahead looking towards the front room, mulling over the incredible events as they had unfolded over the last few days, he was trying desperately to find a clue to the puzzle that he might have missed. His thoughts were interrupted when he noticed a shadow on the blinds of someone crossing his front window, approaching from the right. There was a knock on the door. It was William Barrett.

"Good morning, Mr Gill," he said, twisting his billycock hat in his hands, standing well away from the door. "Have you heard anything of John?"

"Nay. But I've been up to Town Hall and the detectives will be looking after him," Thomas replied.

William Barrett, being economical with words, said no more. He replaced his billycock with both hands and went off to work in the same direction he had arrived. In addition, although it was only a five-minute walk at best, Willie Barrett would not get to work before 7:00 a.m.

Tom Gill returned to his seat and found it peculiar that Barrett, who lived to the left of them, would be coming to see him from the opposite direction. However, he expressed his thoughts to no one, including his increasingly emotional fragile wife.

Eighteen-year-old Joseph Bucke arrived at Back Mellor Street at 7:00 a.m. to clean out Mr. Berwick's stable. He did not have far to go. He lived with his cousin, John Evans, and his wife, Emma, and their two young sons. They all lived at 31 Mellor Street, the same street that backed onto the quiet thoroughfare that housed the stables.

He enjoyed his work as a butcher's apprentice to James Berwick. Berwick was a good man, and one day, Joseph hoped to own a butcher shop of his own. However, one had to start somewhere, which was what Mr. Berwick was always telling him. This was a job that he did not enjoy doing. However, here he was mucking out the stables and yoking the horse, as he did every morning.

Being winter it was still relatively dark, but despite the hour, young Bucke set to work and started mucking out. He had not been at his work long - several minutes, no more, when he noticed a parcel of clothing lying to the left of the coach-house door. It lay in a small recess. He walked over and put the pitchfork into it. The fork met with some resistance. The bundle felt dense.

His curiosity aroused, he took the fork and lifted up the corner of a coat that was lying on top. He wanted to see what was underneath. The lack of natural light was not making it any easier, so he went inside the stable to fetch a lantern. He lit it and placed it on a rusty nail that protruded from the wall. He bent down and removed a little more of the coat to get a better look. As he did so, he gasped, dropped the pitchfork, and recoiled in sheer horror.

His brain was trying desperately to make sense of what his eyes had seen. Then, without choice, his eyes acted like the lens of a camera. They captured the horrific image of a severely mutilated and butchered naked corpse lying in pieces and trussed up in braces. The captured image was seared into his brain so that it would flash before him for days, weeks, months, and finally years to come.

Revulsion consumed him. He rushed into the open and fell over his own feet as he slipped repeatedly on the wet cobblestones, trying desperately to find traction in his haste to escape the atrocious scene.

Joseph Brown Bucke could not read, but he had heard the news of the recent and horrific mutilation of Mary Jane Kelly in Whitechapel, London. He equated what he had heard and what he had now seen to be one and the same. With this in his mind, when he rushed into the street to the bakery next door to raise the alarm, he shouted as he ran, "The Ripper wor here! The Ripper wor here!"

Albert Teale, one of the bakers, stepped out, his hands still covered with flour. He had come out to see what the fracas was about. Young Bucke was running wildly towards him, looking highly agitated.

"Mr. Teale, sir, come sharp! I've found a body at the stables! It's 'orrible, sir! All cut up an' all! I think Jack the Ripper wor 'ere, sir!"

Albert could see that the boy was visibly pale and trembling. He was clearly affected by what he had seen. Suddenly Teale was not too keen to investigate this on his own; despite the fact that he thought the lad was clearly overwrought and probably exaggerating.

By this time, two of the other bakers, James Rastrick and Edward Kirk, had also left their bread and pies to come to investigate the commotion. Teale turned to them and without saying a word jerked his head in the direction of the stables. The three of them quickly fell into step.

When they arrived, Joseph pointed to the bundle lying in the recess. On the second sighting of the butchered body, he left in haste and stood on the cobbled footpath relieving his stomach of its breakfast.

The three men looked at the sight in front of them in silent shocked disbelief.

"Jesus Christ!" exclaimed Teale, who was utterly appalled at what he was looking at. The other two men uttered swear words of their own. They stepped away out into the lane, finding it necessary to remove themselves physically from the bundle of body parts lying on the floor.

"Bucke, go and find a Peeler and come back as soon as you can. An' don't stop and talk to nobody!" Teale ordered, suppressing a wave of nausea. Joseph Bucke turned and fled in search of a police officer. He did not need telling twice.

While waiting for the constables to arrive, the three bakers stood around and spoke in hushed voices. One of them thought he recognised the victim.

People on their way to work had heard the noise and a small gathering soon formed. They all wanted to know what was going on. Teale and the other two men kept them at bay.

"You'll all know soon enough," he said brusquely and left it at that.

P.C. Haigh had been on duty in Manningham Lane and was only a few minutes away from the crime scene when the distressed young Bucke found him and brought him back to the stables. By the time Haigh arrived, a much larger crowd had started to gather, for the news of a murder had spread like wildfire.

The crowd parted to allow the police officer through but soon closed ranks after he had passed. They were fiercely protecting their places while others at the back were jostling for a better position. Everyone was trying to get a better view of the atrocity. Snatches of gossip came down the line from those describing what was up ahead.

P.C. Haigh bent down, holding on to his top hat that had an annoying habit of always slipping off his head, and removed the coat that Teale had strategically replaced to protect the cadaver from prying eyes. However, even he, as a policeman hardened by crime, was shaken to the core by what he saw.

At this point, he did not want to disturb the body in any way. Murder was out of his jurisdiction. He needed to send for his superiors at Town Hall. Albert Teale elected to go as Bucke was still dry retching and in no fit state to go anywhere. Albert Teale swiftly left on foot to relay the tragic tale.

More and more people were joining the throng every minute. Stories of what had happened were fast being passed around as to who had been murdered.

The latest story was that it was Rose, the local prostitute, now horribly mutilated by Jack the Ripper. However, that was soon dispelled when Rose herself turned up to investigate the commotion. Her appearance caused much mirth among the crowd and she immediately demanded to know what was so amusing. When they told her why, through fits of laughter, she did not share their sense of humour. Instead, she left rather miffed, which caused a fresh outbreak of mirth.

As Ruth Gill was walking up Thorncliffe Road on her way to the mill at 8:15 a.m., she could not help but notice people running towards Back Mellor Street. A crowd was so large that it was spilling out onto Thorncliffe Road. There seemed to be a lot of excitement taking place and she was rather curious to see why.

"What's going on?" she asked a man on the edge of the crowd as he stood with one hand in his pocket, drawing hard on a cigarette.

"Best be on your way, lass," he replied in a measured tone. "There is nowt for you here."

Ruth craned her neck down the lane, even standing on tiptoes to try to see what was happening up front, but there were too many tall people blocking her view. With great reluctance, she left the excitement and carried on up the hill. She dare not be late for work.

Ruth was almost at the mill when she met a young acquaintance she worked with but whose name she did not know. This morning they ended up walking up the hill together. After a while, Ruth decided to engage her in conversation.

"Did you see all those folk in Back Mellor Street just now? I wonder what the fuss wor about."

Sally was not sure what to say. Instead, she merely shrugged and remained silent with a troubled mind. When they reached the mill gates some yards later, the girl suddenly stopped.

"It's your John," she finally replied, hardly able to look Ruth in the eye. "John wor murdered."

"Don't talk daft! What a wicked thing to say! If it wor true we would've been told! An' you wouldn't say things like that if you knew how me mam is half mad with worry!"

She was furious with the girl. She wanted to slap her, but her Christian upbringing prevented her from carrying out the burning desire to do so.

How dare she repeat something like that, that wasn't true?

Ruth increased her pace, leaving the girl several steps behind. She was just about to enter the building when she started wondering if perhaps it was true. What if it were? With the seed of doubt taking root she turned, passed the mortified girl on the way down, and retraced her steps to find out for herself.

She entered Thorncliffe Road to see that the gathering numbers had swelled to enormous proportions. There was no way that she would be able to push her way through this crowd that had now blocked up Thorncliffe Road. She stood for a few moments, not sure what to do. She spoke to a woman standing in front of her.

"Excuse me, ma'am," said Ruth tapping her on the shoulder to get her attention. "What happened?"

"It's a murder. A 'orrible murder. They say it's a bad 'un!"

"Who is it?" asked Ruth, fearful of the answer.

"A lad, they say."

Ruth's heart skipped a beat.

"Seventeen or eighteen years of age," the woman continued.

"Thank you, ma'am!"

A wave of relief washed over her at the news. She now had the urge to check to see if Johnny had come home. With dogged determination, Ruth finally managed to elbow her way through the crowd. As she emerged onto the other side, she could not help but notice a small group of people standing around her front door.

Mary Ann came downstairs just after 8:30 a.m. and standing on her toes, kissed her husband's forehead as he stood in front of the kitchen range with Jane. They were trying unsuccessfully to make oatmeal porridge for breakfast. It looked a little like lumpy cement.

"Sit down, Love. Let me do it," she said softly. "I need to keep myself busy."

She had not slept at all. She had spent the night tossing and turning, crying intermittently and fretting about her lad. As a result, she felt thick-headed and a little woolly-brained, but she needed to do something to keep her hands busy.

Tom relinquished the wooden spoon and kissed her tenderly in return. He returned to the table and watched his wife, while Jane remained to see if she could learn some culinary skills.

While they were busy in the kitchen young Samuel was standing on an upturned box looking out of the front room window. He was looking for Johnny. Sammy was missing his older brother badly and wanted him home too. However, while he was looking out the window he noticed that this morning there were more people about than usual. In fact, today many people seemed to be in a great hurry and were rushing up the road. Some were even standing outside his house looking at him through the window.

He dragged the box to the door so that he could open it. He stood on the edge of the footpath, not straying too far from the house. He thought he could see Jane further up the road. He was about to wave to her when he saw

Annie Kershaw coming through the crowd and he focused on her.

However, before she reached Sammy he heard a woman from the group say, "Your poor mam, her Johnny been dead an' all."

Samuel's small mind did not take in the enormity of what the woman had said, but he knew he had to tell his mother. He turned and fled towards the kitchen and in an urgent voice tugged at her skirt repeatedly saying, "Mam! Mam! A lady outside is saying our Johnny is dead!"

Mary Ann froze. She had a bowl in one hand and a spoon in the other. Both remained momentarily suspended in the air. And then they escaped her fingers and crashed onto the flagstone floor. She stood transfixed, unaware of the pottery shards around her feet, the startled child, her shocked husband, or even the small crowd outside her open door. Nor did she see Annie Kershaw moving to support her just as her legs buckled, and before she hit the floor.

Between Annie and Tom, they lowered her into a chair. "They've found a body in Back Mellor Street. Some folk are saying it's Johnny."

Mary Ann grabbed the lace on the front of Annie's dress with both hands in distress. Her face was pale, her lips blue.

"It's not true! It's not true! Annie, tell me it's not true!"

Annie looked at her grief-stricken friend with whom she had spent the last two days of every waking hour searching for the lad. She did not know what to tell Mary

Ann. Instead, she clasped her to her ample bosom and they cried together.

Thomas grabbed his cap and coat and bolted out the door. He pushed his way through the crowd until he came to the stables and coach house. However, a large, strapping policeman barred his path. He towered over Thomas with his black top hat and held a menacing looking truncheon that he repeatedly struck against the open palm of his hand.

"Where do you think you're going in such a hurry then, hey? Get back in line like the rest of 'em!"

Tom stood his ground.

"Please, sir!" Thomas replied quietly, "They tell me you have my lad in there."

Suddenly the demeanour of the policeman changed. He stared at Thomas, looking decidedly uncomfortable. He swallowed twice, cleared his throat, and turned to his superior, who was consulting with his detectives nearby.

"Mr. Dobson, someone here to see you."

Chief Detective-Inspector Dobson left his small circle of investigators. As he walked towards him, Tom noticed that his face was grim.

"Morning, I am Chief Detective-Inspector Dobson, and you are Mr...?"

"Mr. Thomas Gill, sir. Someone tells me you have my lad here. I want to see if it's true."

"Mr. Gill, while I understand your concern I'm afraid that won't be possible. I hope that you can appreciate that we need to do our investigations first. After that, we will take the body by foot ambulance to the mortuary. I suggest you go to the mortuary within the hour and then you'll be able to see if this is your lad or not."

"So it is a lad then? How old is he?"

"I'm very sorry but I'm not at liberty to tell you any more, Mr. Gill."

"Mr. Dobson, please! Can I not just have a look while I'm here? My wife is so distraught about our lad's disappearance that I fear this whole affair will be the very death of her."

"I do understand, but I'm afraid I cannot let you see the body at the moment."

"Put me out of my misery, sir! We've been searching for him for two days an' two nights now, an' we ain't found a trace of him! Please! Just let me take a look while I'm here!"

Thomas Gill, normally calm, placid, and unemotional, was getting increasingly agitated.

The inspector stood his ground.

Joe Thornton, a fellow cabman and friend, had heard Thomas's voice from the fringe and stepped forward. He took him gently by the arm and steered him in the direction of home.

"Let the Peelers do their job, Tom," he said gently. "I'll come with you to the mortuary later on an' hopefully it ain't the lad. No one said that this wor a child. Besides, if it had been your Johnny someone would've come an' told you, you being so close an' all. I'm sure of that."

Arthur Dobson briefed Chief Constable James Withers on the case as soon as he arrived. One would not have called the Chief Constable good looking. He had a round face mostly covered with a mat of thick, grey mutton-chop whiskers and a walrus moustache that all ran into one. The parts of his face that were not covered in facial hair were pasty. His features were rather plain, non-descript - almost forgettable. However, his small, watery, pale blue eyes missed nothing.

With him was Doctor Samuel Lodge, a well-respected police surgeon and medical practitioner who, together with Withers, had arrived as part of the investigation. Samuel Lodge stood quietly for a moment trying to catch his breath. The exertion of the walk, combined with more than five decades of tobacco use, had taken its toll. His corpulent frame was heaving and soft wheezes were escaping from deep within. Now in his 64th year, bespectacled, bald save for a small ring of grey hair clinging tenaciously to the bottom extremities of his head, he too sported large and fearsome mutton chop whiskers.

Within minutes, more detectives arrived on the scene, while another was sent to fetch someone to photograph the body in its surroundings. Preserving images from a crime scene was a relatively new practice and James Withers hoped that they would aid him in his investigation.

While the detectives were making notes of their observations, P.C. Haigh and his colleague were directed by Withers to disperse the now unruly crowd. Chief

Constable James Withers was adamant that this was not going to turn into a three-ring circus.

The detectives set about looking for clues. It was unfortunate that none of them recognized the importance of securing the crime scene or worried about destroying potential evidence as they moved around.

As the fictitious Sherlock Holmes once lamented of a case being investigated in the same era: 'Oh, how simple it would all have been, had I been there, before they came like a herd of buffalo and wallowed all over it.' That was exactly how it was with this murder investigation. Nevertheless, despite their shortcomings, the police were being thorough, and Withers was a stickler for detail. He had trained his team well.

When Doctor Lodge saw the corpse, he was aghast at what he saw. The body was facing away from him lying slightly on its right side, completely nude. The legs had been hacked off with the thighs placed on either side of the head. The feet were protruding behind the back. Other than the fact that his ears had been removed, the throat had not been cut and his face was untouched. Curiously, there was a piece of shirting knotted around the neck, while another piece was found below the trunk, just above the leg stumps. One of the braces was tied around the neck and legs, the other around the trunk.

The body had been eviscerated with a long cut going the full length from the chin to the pubic area. Large portions of the intestines had been displaced and were draped around the neck. The heart had been ripped out and stuck under the chin. He noticed two small puncture wounds on the chest. The lungs were missing, and in their place, a pair of boots were shoved into the open chest cavity. Finally, Lodge noted as he turned the body over, the penis, anus had been carved out, and these too appeared to be missing.

He checked the clothes, and although they all seemed to be accounted for, he would need to double-check this with the next of kin later. Lodge had found some of the lad's clothes on the ground underneath his body and other clothing items had been placed on the top. The body parts were sandwiched in between. On further examination, there was no knife damage to any of the items of clothing. He deduced then that the deceased must have been naked when he was stabbed.

The only blood at the scene was to the edge of his hat, which looked as if it had become soaked after falling into a pool of blood. There were also some slight markings on the collar that could have been blood. Other than that, the clothes were spotlessly clean.

In addition, that was not the only thing that was clean.

On closer inspection, Lodge realized that not only had the body been drained of every last drop of blood, but it had also been thoroughly washed, inside and out. The corpse was incredibly clean. He estimated that this would have taken at least an hour to perform. He had never seen anything like it.

Had the body been drained of blood and washed for easy transportation, to prevent blood drips as it was being transported? Alternatively, had the body been washed to remove any contamination of evidence?

He found it all rather baffling.

As soon as Chief Constable James Withers had seen the gruesome scene, he too was visibly shaken. He had been a policeman for nearly thirty years and he had never seen anything so horrific and disturbing. He looked at the body chopped up and parcelled like something found in a butcher shop ready for delivery. It was time to call his team over.

"Men, gather round. I want you to have a good look at what you see before you and then ask yourselves questions, because we're not dealing with your usual killer here."

They left what they were doing and stood around him in a semi-circle. The corpse was still lying in the recess with Withers standing to the right of it. Most that stood there were feeling rather queasy and preferred not to focus on the body but fixed their eyes on Withers, instead.

"Gentlemen, as usually we will be looking at this case as objectively as possible, and at the same time I want you to question everything you see. I want to ask you this. Who do we have living in our midst that would treat a body with such disrespect? Killing was not enough for him, neither was the act of mutilation. The urge was to kill, mutilate, and then display the body in a most gruesome fashion. Displaying a body like this is with the intent to shock and disturb.

"Ask yourselves, was the body dismembered because of some perverse pleasure or was it done for pure convenience?"

"Apart from removing his ears the lad's face is untouched. Why? Is this how the killer wanted to remember him? On the other hand, was his face not disfigured so that we would know who he was?

He looked critically at the crime scene.

"I am sure that by now you have noticed that there is a distinct lack of blood and general disturbance here. This is evidently the secondary crime scene. We need to find out where the primary crime scene is, and my guess is that it won't be too far away.

"Let's think logically for a minute. The perpetrator kills but needs to dispose of the body. He can't just put it in a cab and take it somewhere so he decides to cut it up, to make it smaller for better transportation. If that being the case, then one would assume that either the killer lives nearby, or the crime was committed very close to this dumping ground.

"I say that because of the way the body was packaged. It is too bulky to have been transported in a portmanteau. It is possible that it was brought here on foot, perhaps disguised as just a large parcel or a bundle of old clothes. Risky, but possible.

"Yet one cannot carry something like this over a long distance without being noticed, even if done at the dead of night. No doubt, they would have been fearful of meeting one of our men on the beat or the possibility of losing a body part during transportation.

"The body was secured by braces together with the various items of clothing. However, there is no real security here. No string, rope, or belt that would have done a better job. In many respects, this crime seems to have been very well planned, but when you look at the way the body was secured, one has to wonder if the crime was as well planned as it first appears.

"Was this then a premeditated crime that was poorly executed? Was the body left here because the killer needed to get rid of it fast? Were his plans interrupted? What was the cause, if they were? On the other hand, just maybe this was the intended dumping ground all along because it has some significance for the killer.

"Also, the timeframe of when the body could have been left here is very narrow. Talking to the constable on this beat, we know that that the body was left here sometime between 4:35 a.m. and 7:00 a.m. this morning. We also know that those working in the mills would have been out on the streets from 5:00 a.m.

"As I mentioned before, carrying something like this is difficult to do unnoticed and the additional time taken to display the body would have been risky. Time that could have meant the difference of being detected or not. Unless of course the killer is familiar with people's movements in the area and he was confident that he had the time to carry out the deed.

"How many of you have noticed the house opposite? Number 12 Mellor Street, I believe. I'm told by the same constable that they always have their light on at night. This means that during the night the light from the upper windows shines directly into this recess. So gentlemen, why would someone who was trying to conceal a body place it in an area bathed with light when there were other spots along this lane far less conspicuous?

"This is a dark little thoroughfare most of the time and not well used at all. Tradesmen use most of these buildings for storage. Who would know that this lane exists, and for what purpose, other than someone with local knowledge? We need to be looking for someone who is from the area or even closer to home, perhaps from the immediate Manningham neighbourhood.

"Which brings me to my next point, gentlemen. Now I am aware that Bradford has already been abuzz with rumours saying that this is the work of Jack the Ripper. I don't want you to be swayed in any way by this. There is a possibility that this is indeed the work of the East London fiend, and we will have to make inquiries to confirm or refute this. However, my first thoughts are that someone committed this crime with a real knowledge of the area. I also feel that the crime was carried out in such a way that the killer wanted us to think that this was the work of Jack the Ripper, thereby creating a decoy to discourage us from looking closer to home.

"Why do I say that? I want you all to pay attention men, as I am sure that you are all familiar by now with the unfortunate slaying of Mary Jane Kelly in London recently. Knowing the case, look carefully at how the killer has displaced and strategically displayed various parts of the organs of the body. They have mimicked many of her injuries.

"Is there any significance of the white shirting around the neck? Is this a sign? Does it echo other victims from the East End? Is this something we have seen on other victims in the area? We find it again on the leg stumps. It has no bearing on keeping the body intact so we have to ask ourselves what this could mean. What is the significance of this for the killer? Have we seen anything like this in past cases? In other unsolved murders? Is there anything here that you recognize, no matter how small?

"Remember, we have to look at a crime scene in layers, gentlemen. Peel them back, one by one, for it is not always as it seems."

Although his men always referred to him as 'Owd Withers' behind his back, it was this profound insight that he had when visiting crime scenes that earned him their respect.

As for Doctor Lodge, he had stood with the detectives in silence, listening to his colleague and nodding his head from time to time. After the briefing, he was heard to say, as an aside to Withers, that the state of the body was the most revolting spectacle he had ever seen, with the bones and the flesh hacked at in the most merciless manner.

For those that were there, few would have disagreed. For this would be a case that none of them would ever forget.

Thomas Gill, together with his good friend Joe, stood in the cold mortuary corridor to see if the murdered victim was Johnny.

Thomas was too preoccupied with his thoughts to engage in conversation. He was struggling to suppress emotions that he feared would betray him as soon as he opened his mouth. Joseph, who was a man who did not believe in small talk, spent the time puffing away on a cigarette while they stood in mutual silence.

Eventually, a side-door opened and Doctor Samuel Lodge emerged wearing a stained apron. He looked at both men and said, "Which one of you is Mr. Gill?"

Thomas stepped forward and they shook hands.

"Mr. Gill, I believe you wish to see a body we brought in this morning. We'll bring you into the autopsy room and you'll be able to see it for yourself. You may bring your friend in, if you wish. If you identify the body as one of your own then we'll need to talk further. Are you ready?"

Thomas was not ready. What parent would be? He was praying, hoping that when he walked into that room, it would not be his Johnny lying on the slab.

With great reluctance and trepidation, he followed the police surgeon into the room. They entered the well-lit autopsy room that smelled faintly of thymol and carbolic acid and something else Tom could not quite place. He did not notice much else of the room itself; neither the instruments nor the embalming fluids and other chemicals in jars placed neatly side-by-side on a nearby shelf. Instead, his eyes were fixed only on the small mound covered with a thin, white sheet. His heart beat faster. It was pulsating in his throat. His hands were sweating.

Please God! Don't let it be Johnny! Please God! Don't let it be Johnny!

The doctor moved to the table and started to withdraw the sheet. The first thing he saw was a mop of golden curls. He drew a sharp breath and held it there. More sheeting was removed to reveal the face in its entirety. Lodge tucked the remainder of the material firmly under the chin.

Thomas's vision was filled with a beautiful, fair-haired child. His eyes were edged with dark, long lashes that were closed, resting on his small rounded cheeks. He looked as if he were sleeping. He stared at the child. He closed his eyes. He opened them again and when he spoke, his voice cracked.

"It's our Johnny," he whispered.

Silence hung in the room. Poignant. Palpable. Time suspended. Then the realisation hit full force.

"It's our Johnny!" he said a little louder.

The exclamation was of disbelief mixed with raw emotion of recognition.

"Oh, God! No! Oh! Oh! Oh!" The last three words were punctuated with heavy, laboured breathing and wracking sobs.

Thomas Gill's life as he knew it changed in a hair's breadth of a second. His very soul was tortured at the sight of his beautiful boy lying lifeless on the cold mortuary slab.

His boy. His boy who would laugh no more. Who would never entertain his boss and fellow cabmen with snatches of recited poetry learned from school that used to swell his heart with pride. No more teasing and ruffling his hair. No more dreams for his future. A life cut down; finished. Snuffed out like a candle. Here one minute, gone the next.

Tom Gill was overwhelmed with the blackness of grief. He was beyond grief-stricken. His raw pain and grief were horrible to watch. The doctor dragged a chair towards him and Tom fell back into it, unaware of anything going on around him.

Lodge often witnessed people grieving. It came with the job. Watching a parent openly grieve for their dead child never made it any easier.

However, it was what he knew, that of which he would have to tell this father who clearly loved this child, it was this that was going to be a very difficult thing to do, even for someone like him who had become relatively desensitized dealing with death on a daily basis.

He averted his eyes as Thomas Gill placed his head in his hands and continued to weep openly and bitterly. He waited for the man to compose himself and eventually he said, "Mr. Gill, please come into my office."

Joseph supported Thomas and took him into the room for more privacy.

Doctor Lodge looked over the rim of his steel-framed glasses at both men sitting opposite him while he shuffled some papers on his desk. He spoke after a minute or two.

"Mr. Gill, I am truly sorry for the loss of your child. I am even sorrier to have to tell you that there are extensive injuries to the body. This crime has been carried out in a particularly brutal manner, the like I have never encountered before. If you wish, due to how upset you clearly are, we can discuss these tomorrow."

Thomas declined. He needed to know what had happened to his boy. When he listened to the doctor describing what had been done to Johnny he felt as if his heart would shatter into a million pieces.

He listened as to how he had first been stabbed above and below the heart. How the body had been mutilated, butchered, washed, drained, and finally packaged and left just yards from his house.

What sort of monster would do that to a child? His child?

The question remained unasked and he wept again as he listened. The agony was unbearable.

Finally, he managed to ask one question.

"Doctor, how quick did the lad go?"

"Mr. Gill, the first stabbing severed the major arteries and his death would've been quick. The mutilations took place well after death."

It was not much, but Thomas took some small comfort in knowing this. This was not to last long. Not after what the police surgeon told him next.

"Mr. Gill, unfortunately, there is something else."

Thomas wondered what more he could possibly tell him after having listened to the doctor speak of such dreadful atrocities,

Lodge drew a breath and cleared his throat. He shuffled some more papers, buying time before continuing.

"Both Doctor Major and I are under the impression that an outrage was committed on your son before or after death. However, we cannot be sure, because the whole of his penis and anus were cut away and these were not found at the crime scene. More than likely they were removed to hide any evidence of such a thing taking place."

Thomas was appalled. He questioned the surgeon to verify what he had just heard.

"An outrage, sir? Talk plain. Do you mean my boy was raped?"

Doctor Lodge hesitated, cleared his throat and replied, "Mr. Gill, due to the nature of this crime and looking at motive and the missing body parts, we believe that it is a strong possibility."

Thomas sat there stunned. He felt a surge of deep rage.

If I ever find the person responsible, I will kill him. I will kill him with my own bare hands. My poor Johnny! How he must have suffered so! Oh, my God! I can't tell any of this to Mary Ann; it will kill her for sure. How am I even going to tell her Johnny is dead?

"Mr. Gill, I hope you don't mind me asking, but this has been a shocking murder. The stabbings were done with such intense force that it seems that the crime was carried out in great anger. Do you have any idea who may have committed such a crime? Is there anyone you can think of that may have a grudge against either you or your family? Someone you may suspect?"

Thomas was feeling dissociated from his surroundings. Everything felt surreal. The last revelation was beyond his ability to think clearly.

Enemies? He racked his brain, but could not think of anyone who would want to harm his lad or himself.

"No, sir, I'm at a loss as to who would wish to do this terrible, terrible thing to us. I can't think of anyone," he said, finally.

"What about Barrett?"

"Barrett?" Thomas snapped his head up and asked incredulously, "Willie Barrett?"

Doctor Lodge nodded in affirmation.

"My God! No! Surely not! The boy and Barrett were friends. The lad enjoyed his company and Barrett his."

"Well, Mr. Gill," said Lodge, standing up to indicate that the meeting was over, "I extend my sincere condolences to you and your wife. It has been a terrible shock, I know. Hopefully, the constabulary will find the killer soon and bring him to justice."

Both men stood up and shook his hand. Joe, who had sat in silence listening to the doctor speak, had been shocked at what he had heard. He could not even begin to imagine what Thomas must be going through.

"Thank you, sir. Can I ask when we can take our Johnny home to bury him?"

Doctor Lodge followed them to the door, paused and placed a hand on Tom's shoulder.

"Mr. Gill, may I call you Thomas?" He nodded. "Thomas, you don't want to see your lad how he is. No father should have to see these horrible mutilations and neither should your wife.

"Doctor Major, Mr. Miall and I also need to carry on examining the body for other possible clues and this will take some time. Once we release the body we suggest that you allow the undertakers to deal with the remains so that he can then be buried accordingly."

Thomas reluctantly agreed but he wanted one more thing before he left.

"Doctor Lodge, can we please have a lock of Johnny's hair? I know my wife would want it."

He followed the doctor back into the room where Johnny lay looking so peaceful. He was as bonny in death as he had been in life and this made it even more difficult to come to terms with the fact that he was dead.

Tom walked over to his son and brushed his curls back from his forehead with his hand, just as he had done in the kitchen just three mornings prior. However, this time he stroked his hair more gently. He remembered how happy they had been that morning, drinking their tea around the table, laughing and joking. His heart ached at the memory. He bent down, and cradling Johnny's head gently in his left hand; he kissed him for the last time on the lips. Lips that were lifeless, cold, unresponsive.

Doctor Lodge came over with the small pair of scissors he had been looking for and snipped a lock of hair from the nape of the neck. He carefully tied the hair with a piece of yellow ribbon and presented it to Thomas.

Thomas took the lock and placed it onto the palm of his hand. He curled his fingers around it and squeezed it tightly. His eyes welled up once more. Through a veil of unchecked tears, he bid the surgeon goodbye and took his leave, but not before securing the lock of hair inside his inner coat pocket and placing it against his beating heart.

Joe and Thomas parted company soon afterwards, with Thomas going to explain to his boss, Mr. Whittaker, why he would need more time off work.

Whittaker was shocked when he heard the news because he knew Johnny well. He had been one of the men Johnny would regularly entertain at the cabstand in Manningham Lane. He had been more than fond of the boy.

"Oh! My God, Thomas! How awful! I'm extremely sorry to hear this, Tom. I was right fond of your lad, as you know. He was a very special 'un. Please pass on my condolences to Mary Ann and let me know when the funeral will be," he said, putting a comforting arm around Thomas's shoulders as he walked him to the door.

"And don't worry about your wages. I'll pay you in full come the end of the month. You take as much time off as you need. This is truly a horrible business. Tragic! Just tragic!"

He left Thomas shaking his head in disbelief as he walked back to his office.

Telling Mr. Whittaker why he could not come back to work just yet was hard enough, but having to tell Mary Ann that the lad was dead, that was the part he was dreading the most.

As he walked home each step felt as if his feet were made of lead. He walked the route, head bowed, deep in thought as he let his mind wander to a much happier day when Johnny had been born.

He could remember it as if it were yesterday. They were still living in the tiny house in Bolton Road situated on the ridge that had a pretty view overlooking the town from the top rooms. It sat snugly in a long row of other houses, all side-by-side, closely abutted, all looking the same. Nevertheless, they were happy there.

Ruth had been born first, with Jane coming two years later. He was right chuffed when his children started to arrive. He was a young father, a very young father, but both his girls had been born healthy, and more importantly, Mary Ann had not been in any danger. He could not deny that when the midwife informed him one dreary day on 5th February that the child that he could hear drawing its first breath and airing its little lungs was a boy, the day had become considerably brighter.

He had bounded up the stairs two at a time and had incurred the wrath of the buxom midwife following hard behind him, puffing and panting as she tried to keep up. She had not quite finished getting Mary Ann ready for him and she tried to prevent him from entering as they reached the room. However, he did not care. He just wanted to kiss his bonny lass and see his new bairn.

With a vexed look, the fearsome midwife, still breathing heavily, presented him with his lad. And beautiful he was! He was perfect! He cradled his small miracle and took him over to the window to get a better look at him. As he did so, the child stopped crying. He looked at Thomas intensely with the deepest of blue eyes, took his index finger, and clutched it firmly within his tiny grasp.

Tom's heart lurched as he sensed a joy never felt before. He bent down, kissed him on the crown of his head, and brought him back to his mother. Kissing his wife tenderly on the brow, still damp from exertion, he placed the baby carefully into her waiting arms.

"Thank you, Mary Ann! Thank you! What a gift we have here!" She smiled up at him, pleased that she had finally managed to produce a son that she knew he had wanted for so long, though he had not said.

The baby started to mewl again. She unbuttoned her nightdress and put him to her breast. He suckled noisily and greedily. Mary Ann looked down at her new baby in total adoration as Tom left the room quietly, closing the door softly behind him.

Thomas could see a throng of people milling around his house from the top of the rise. As he neared, he saw some he knew and others he did not. They fell away in silence on his approach; his face telling them what they already knew.

No sooner had he closed the door than Mary Ann left her seat. She crossed the space between them in an instant. The anguish of waiting to hear whether the body in the stable was her Johnny had been unbearable. She grabbed the lapels of his coat, and hanging onto them started asking him frantically, "Please, Tom! Please tell me it ain't our Johnny they found! Please!"

She was shocked to see his tortured expression. She watched him struggling desperately; trying to reach deep for words that would not come. In the end, he embraced her tightly saying, "I'm sorry, lass, I'm sorry. I'm right sorry."

She gasped audibly. The pain was excruciating. It was if an iron weight was pressing hard onto her chest. She could not breathe. Her body trembled uncontrollably. Her heart raced. Despite the cold, beads of sweat broke out on her upper lip and her hands began to sweat. Her breathing became more and more rapid until she felt that her very lungs were smothering her, choking her, denying her oxygen. Her knees buckled and she uttered a heart-wrenching primeval wail that seemed to go on forever.

Thomas was at a loss on how to comfort her. He wanted to take away her pain but his own pain was all consuming too. Feeling utterly useless, he sat on the floor with her and cradled her in his arms. Her distress did not abate. In fact, it escalated. Soon her grief bordered on hysteria.

Thomas was becoming increasingly worried. Finally, he picked her up off the floor and placed her gently on the sofa. Leaving her with Annie Kershaw and several other woman friends who were standing around quietly weeping, Tom went in dire haste to fetch the doctor to give her something to soothe her nerves and ease her pain. An opiate at this stage seemed the only remedy. He wished at that moment that he too could have something to numb the senses and block the pain. He just wanted to escape from the nightmare that without warning had followed and engulfed them both.

The doctor was duly found and brought back to the house. After a dose of Batley's sedative solution, for the first time in 36 hours his Mary Ann closed her eyes and started to look more relaxed. He saw the doctor out, as well as all the remaining women, and returned to sit on the edge of the sofa to be with her. He took her tiny hand in his and watched her tear-stained face as her chest rose and fell, a little sob occasionally escaping, until at last she drifted off into a deep, rhythmic sleep.

The events of the last few days seemed to have stretched into eternity. As hope had ebbed, shock, disbelief, and numbness had surged to take its place. His heart ached at the knowledge he alone was burdened to know.

As she slept, he let down his guard once again and he wept. He held her hand to his cheek as the tears streamed unrestrained, and the pangs in his chest returned at the thought that his lad, his bonny lad, the lad he loved more than life itself, was now no more.

The children, on hearing the unfamiliar noise of their father crying, now hovered at the door. Their mother's grief had frightened them, but seeing their father cry was shocking. He had always been their pillar of strength. It was he they went to for comfort, when they scraped their knees or bumped their heads. Ruth was uncertain as to whether she should comfort him or close the door. In the end, she closed the door and ushered the rest of the crying children into another room.

Eventually, Thomas composed himself. He wiped his eyes, blew his nose and gazed at his wife's serene countenance. Her bloom of youth had long gone but she was still beautiful to him. She continued to sleep deeply, oblivious to his pain and distress. He kissed the tips of her fingers of the hand that was still in his and pressed them against his wet cheek.

"Mary Ann! Mary Ann!" he said in a quiet, but urgent voice. "What are we going to do now without wee Johnny?"

Withers and his team were still working the crime scene. He called them together and spoke to them out of earshot of another wave of ghoulish onlookers who had appeared just as they had managed to disperse the last ones.

"Men, it would appear that the body now taken up to the mortuary is that of young John Gill, the lad that was reported missing by his parents in the early hours of Friday morning. The father identified him earlier today.

"According to him, when he made the missing person's report, the lad was last seen in the company of a man named William Barrett. Apparently, Barrett works as the local milkman for a Mr. John Wolfenden at Ashfield Dairies on Manningham Lane. They stable their horse at 11 Belle Vue.

"When you have finished gathering evidence here, Constable Haigh I want you to ask those that were first on the scene to come to the station to make a statement. That includes P.C. Kirk, Albert Teale, his colleagues, and young Joseph Bucke.

"I also want you to go down to 24 Bateman Street and bring Barrett in for questioning. Then go to Ashfield Dairies and get hold of his employer Wolfenden. Tell him we want to have a look at his stables in Belle Vue. I also want an investigation done at the Ashfield Dairy. See what you can find. I want no stone unturned."

After Haigh had left, Chief Constable Withers surveyed the scene once more. He was looking for the smallest of clues, making sure that they had missed nothing. However, while he stood there looking at the site in reflection, he could not help but wonder about the irony of the perpetrator's choice for a dumping ground. A butchered child left at the door of a butcher's stable. Was it coincidence, or again a place carefully chosen for impact, shock, and effect? In addition, the fact that the boy was found yards from his home was something James also felt was done with calculating intent.

Something else struck him while he was standing there. Today was Innocents Day, a holy day commemorating the massacre of the boys by King Herod while trying to kill the infant Jesus.

Bastard! This is one sick, bloody bastard.

A couple of hours later James Withers sat back at his desk and started reading the statements that were waiting for him, just as he had asked. His eyes began to water again. They were rebelling against the enormous paperwork his job involved. He should have had glasses by now, but there was never enough time to have his eyes tested. Work always took precedence.

He picked up the first statement. It was from P.C. Kirk, who had been on duty in Mellor Street on Friday night and a good part of Saturday morning. Kirk stated that he had tried the doors to the Berwick stable and coach house at half-past four on the Saturday morning, and had found them locked. He also said that he had stood on the very spot where they had found the body and it was definitely not there at that time. The three bakers corroborated his timelines, whose statements he read next. He read the statement of Mrs. Annie Kershaw and that of Ruth Gill, but neither told him anything of importance.

He then read the statement made by Joseph Bucke, who had discovered the body.

'I am employed by Mr. James Berwick of the Market Hall, who has a stable and coach-house in Thorncliffe Road, near to where I found the body.

'I was there last Friday night about 9:00 p.m. but saw nothing unusual at the time. On Saturday morning, I went to the stable, as usual, to look after Mr. Berwick's horse. That was a little before 7:00 a.m. I went into the stable and after attending to the horse, I took some manure out into the yard in front of the coach-house, where there is a manure pit. I had thrown the manure in when I saw a heap of something propped up in the corner, between the wall and the coach-house door. I could not make out what it was at the time, so I got a light and then saw that it was a dead body. I noticed that one ear was cut off.

'I was alarmed and went for a man in the bake house close by. He saw the boy, and I went for a policeman. I soon found one. He saw the body, and I then went to fetch a doctor, who came and saw the body. I noticed that the body was tied up in a jacket or some piece of clothing with a leather belt or something strapped around it. I stopped about the place for some time but did not care to look at the body. I don't know how it was cut up or injured.'

After reading several more statements that were on his desk, he sent for Haigh to bring in William Barrett, who had arrived some minutes before.

"Thank you for coming in, Mr. Barrett. We are hoping that you can help in our investigations of the murder of young Johnny Gill. You knew the boy apparently." He paused, waiting and watching Barrett like a hawk.

Barrett showed no emotion. He also seemed strangely unaffected by the news that the lad he had known well was dead. He replied rather indifferently that he had known the boy and that he had heard that he had been killed.

"Mr. Barrett, we understand that you were the last person to be seen with the lad. At what time did he leave you and where?"

"I wor in Walmer Villas, just before half eight when the lad says he wants to go home for his breakfast. I wor one stop away from the milk round, an' usually he waits until I'm finished. But this time he didn't, and so he left."

"Are you sure that you did not have the boy with you at a later stage?"

"Yes, sir! Quite sure!"

Withers took a gamble. He shuffled the witness statements that he had just read in front of him. He held one up. The fact that it was Joseph Bucke's statement was of no importance.

"Mr. Barrett, what if I tell you that we have a witness who is prepared to swear that the Gill lad was still with you much later than the hour you are suggesting. What do you say now?"

Barrett cast his eyes to the ground. There was a pregnant pause.

"Perhaps he wor with me until 9:30 a.m. or so. Maybe even later. But he definitely left me at Walmer Villas."

Withers was like a bloodhound. He knew that he was on the right trail.

"So Mr. Barrett, from what I have been told, your typical route is to finish the first part of your round at Walmer Villas, go back to the dairy and then start the second round on another route. So why would you have gone back to Walmer Villas when you had already completed your deliveries there?"

Barrett remained silent.

"Mr. Barrett, we'll be holding you here until we do a thorough search of your house. Do you have a problem with that?"

"None whatsoever," he said, quite confidently, trying to stifle a yawn.

Withers admired his calm exterior. He was either a master at hiding his feelings or he was an entirely innocent man who had nothing to hide. He had not made up his mind as to which he was yet, but he would, before the day was out.

With Barrett detained, Withers called his three senior detectives, King, Abbey, and Butterworth, into his office.

"Gentlemen, I do believe Barrett is our man. I want you to go down to the Barrett household and do a thorough search for the possible murder weapon. Doctor Lodge has already indicated that the knife used on the lad was very specific, the details of which I'll give you later. Nevertheless, I also want you to look for any other evidence that you can find that will strengthen our case. In addition, while you're doing that, I'll be trying to find as many eyewitnesses as possible. I'll also go over to Thorncliffe Road to interview the parents."

Within an hour after Barrett was summoned to the police station to help with their investigation, the detectives arrived at his home. They searched it thoroughly.

The murder weapon had been quite distinctive, according to Doctor Lodge. The knife used in the crime had not been that sharp, as the flesh had been crudely hacked and very unskilfully. They were looking for a knife that had a blade width of one and a half inches, and a length of eight inches. More importantly, the blade would be wider at the base and the tip would have a distinct curve.

Detective King walked into the kitchen and started looking around. He failed to see any knives on display.

"Could we see your kitchen knives, Mrs Barrett?" he asked.

In a drawer were two knives of the same width they were looking for. One of the knives stood out. It was of particular interest. Not only did it have the same blade width of one and a half inches but it also had a length of eight inches. However, more significantly, the blade was broader at the base than at the tip, which ended in an unusual curve.

Detective King examined it with great interest. He took it to the window so that he could cast a better light on it. He looked at the hilt and the blade itself. He noticed that although there had been an attempt to clean the knife it had been hurriedly done. On the tip of the knife were some dark stains - unusual for a breadknife. He turned to Margaret Barrett who was hovering in the background.

"Mrs. Barrett when last was this knife cleaned?"

"It wor cleaned at the end of this week, sir, with the rest of the silverware."

"What is this knife used for?"

"For cutting bread."

Detective King took possession of the knife, and they went on with their search. They entered the bedroom. On the bed was a large blue and gold, well-used carpetbag, the once pretty patterns now worn away with canvas showing through in patches. It was half packed.

"Going somewhere, Mrs. Barrett?"

"I'm taking the baby and going to stay with my people in Cononley until all this is over and Willie is released."

Detective King admired her optimism but did not respond.

After further searching, several items were recovered. One was of notable interest. They found a pair of black worsted trousers and a sleeved, full-length waistcoat, both of which were cold and damp as if they had been recently washed.

"Did you launder these recently, Mrs Barrett?" asked Detective King holding up the waistcoat and the pair of trousers.

"I can't remember, sir. I may have."

"Mrs. Barrett, what time did your husband come home on Friday night?"

"I think it wor just after ten thirty. Perhaps ten thirty-five."

"Does he usually come home at that time of the night after work?"

"Nay, he's usually home by eight, but he told me that he'd to churn butter for Mr. Wolfenden that evening for Saturday Market, an' so he'd to work late."

"Did he leave the house at any time after he returned home on Thursday or Friday night?"

"Nay, sir, he wor here with me, like he always is."

"Thank you, Mrs. Barrett, for your time. You do understand that we'll have to take these to the station for examination," he said, pointing to the clothes and knife.

"Aye, sir, I do. I just want my Willie home."

With the knife and clothes in hand, they went back to the police station to present them to the Chief Constable. After that, they went on to pay Mr. Wolfenden a visit to verify William Barrett's milk run route and hours worked.

The detectives were told that they could have free access to the Wolfenden stables, and for this, they were grateful. Many times during their investigations people often obstructed their searches and made their jobs every difficult.

The first thing Detective King did when he arrived was to make a note of its location in relation to the other surrounding buildings. The stable was directly opposite the back of the Servants' Home. It looked as if some bedrooms that backed onto the courtyard were occupied. Hopefully, someone might have seen or heard something of interest over the last few nights. He made a mental note of telling Withers so that they could send one of his colleagues over later to interview the occupants.

When he looked at the construction of the stable, he saw that the façade was made entirely of wood, except for a horizontal panel of windows up at the top. Although the panels were too high to see into at street level, perhaps someone had seen a light coming from the stables or had noticed some unusual activity. This was something else he would need to follow up.

He moved inside and looked at the layout. The stable itself was not that big - about 12 square yards. There were two stalls, one of which was used for the horse. The other was for storage. At the bottom of the stalls was a channel, which led to a sink near a water tap. An iron grating covered the sink. He could not help notice that the floor was very wet.

While he was looking at the layout, his colleagues were searching for clues among the straw-strewn floor. He went over to them.

"What have you found so far, Butterworth?"

"Not, a lot, I have to say. We did find this, however." He got up off his haunches and retrieved a wrapper or coarse canvas that had some dark brown stains on it. In addition, a bag that they had retrieved had also been hidden from view. On one side of the bag, the words 'W. Mason, Derby-road, Liverpool' could be clearly seen.

"Blood?" asked King, looking at the canvas, his eyes still trying to adjust to the dark light in the barn.

"I'm not sure, but the stains are placed in such a way that it looks as if something has been placed or laid on top of it. It's also quite moist."

"Where did you find these?"

"They were secreted underneath some hay bales in the horse stall."

"What else have you found?"

"Well, did you notice all the water on the floor when you came in?"

"Yes, I did. Quite a large amount of water."

"Yes, it is all rather strange. Have a look here." With that, he brought King back to the middle of the stable and pointed to the floor, drawing his attention back to the wet floor.

Three-quarters of the floor of the stable between the sink and the channel was very wet. It looked as if it had recently been washed and scrubbed, as there was a considerable amount of water still lying about, the rest of which had drained into a central point between the two stalls. Under the tap in the stable sat a can of clean water. As they moved from there to the neighbouring stall where the horse was kept, it was surprisingly bone dry.

"Yes, all rather odd, I agree. Good work on finding the coarse canvas. We'll need to have some analysis done on what has been found to date. And I am beginning to think that we will need to check these drains."

He turned to his other detectives. "Detective Sergeant Abbey I want you to go over to Bridge Street and ask Mr. Rimmington if he can come over. I do believe that his expert opinion will be of value to this investigation. See if he will agree to come right away."

They were an hour into their investigation and the only bit of potential evidence they had found so far was the coarse canvas and the bag. Overall, he was frustrated. Everything looked so clean, too clean. Especially considering it was a stable.

Someone had been busy trying to clean up any evidence, and most successfully. He just hoped that if the body had been dismembered here he would find some evidence of blood or remnants of flesh in the drains. He hoped that the cleaning up had not been a complete success.

"Ah, Mr. Rimmington, sir. Thank you for coming." The spry Mr. Rimmington had finally arrived and he shook Detective King's hand warmly. They had worked several cases together.

Felix Marsh Rimmington was the borough analyst with a chemist in Bridge Street. He had worked closely with the police on a number of cases. As a result, his colleagues respected him for his scientific approach. He was still riding the crest of the wave of the infamous Humbug Billy case he had solved thirty years prior. His reputation preceded him.

"I wondered when you lads were going to call me down here," he said with a twinkle in his eye. "I'd hardly opened my chemist this morning before I was being told of this dreadful affair by half of Manningham. Of course, each story I heard became progressively worse and in the end, I was quite sure that what I was hearing was entirely fanciful. So what are the facts then?"

Rimmington, no longer in his prime, stroked his grey beard several times as Detective King spoke. He looked at him through the rounded lenses of his glasses that aided eyes now weakened through years of close work. He listened intently. When King was finished, he was appalled. He realised then that the gruesome and grotesque stories that he had earlier disregarded as fanciful gossip, were in the main, true.

Chief Constable James Withers lost no time in gathering evidence against William Barrett. In fact, he had been an extremely busy man. He had visited Margaret Barrett to see how much she knew and to find out about her husband's movements over the last few days. He then retraced Barrett's steps to determine the length and time it would take him to go from his home to work and from the stables back to his home. He had interviewed Thomas and Mary Ann, several of Barrett's neighbours, and put out the word that he was looking for any witnesses who could help him in his investigation.

When he got back to the police station, he decided to confront Barrett with the evidence he had gathered so far and to see what he had to say for himself. Barrett was duly brought out of his cell and now sat opposite Withers, a desk between them.

Withers looked at him with disdain. He wanted to give the man a fair trial, but could not help listen to the stories from his men that Barrett appeared unusually unaffected by both the boy's death and his detention. Considering he had known the lad quite well, he found his attitude rather callous. His men had also told him that while being detained in his cell, Barrett seemed entirely unaffected by his position. In fact, he was rather upbeat and jovial, laughing and joking with the policemen on duty and often bursting into song.

Something else they said that struck a chord was that Barrett had been yawning rather excessively. Without any further prompting, Barrett yawned just at that moment and continued to do so throughout their interview.

"Mr. Barrett, I'm going to ask you a few questions and show you some items that we have collected from your house and place of work."

Barrett nodded his head.

"Can you tell me who you work for, how long you have been there, and describe your typical working day."

"I work at the Ashfield Dairy at 200 Manningham Lane for Mr. Wolfenden. I've been there just a few weeks, having come from Kildwick. However, I used to work for Mr. Wolfenden at the Ashfield farm in Cross Hills as a farm labourer, before working for him here in Bradford.

"My duties, along with the other boys, are to deliver milk during the day, an' in addition to that, I've to work the cream extractor an' help with making butter in my spare time.

"I'm expected to be up at the Belle Vue stables by 6:30 a.m. to feed an' groom the horse. I then nip on home to my house in Bateman Street for breakfast, nip on back to the stable in time to harness the horse an' get down to the station in time to meet the milk train.

"After giving the two milk boys employed by the dairy their supply of milk in hand cans, I then drive a short round delivering milk to a few early customers an' then I'm due back at the dairy at about nine.

"Once I've delivered the surplus milk at the dairy, I then start another round, which is usually completed at 11:00 at a house behind Lister's Mill. I then come back to the stable an' put up the horse, work the cream extractor, or do any other jobs needed. I've to be back at the station again by 5:40 to meet the train for the evening milk, an' on my return, I nip on to the dairy an' take my turn at the extractor. I'm occupied at the dairy till a little after 8:00 in the evening."

"We went to our house today and found this," said Withers, producing the knife and placing it on the table between them.

Withers watched Barrett closely for any reaction. There was not a flicker of recognition.

"Do you recognize this knife, Barrett?"

"Nay, sir. Should I? I've never seen that knife before."

"Never? Let me say, that we retrieved this knife from your kitchen, Barrett. It matches the stab wounds found on the child perfectly."

For the first time Barrett did not look so self-assured. He shuffled in the hard, wooden chair, repositioning himself and stifled a yawn.

"Well, perhaps it's similar to the one my wife bought for the bread. But I cannot say for sure that it is the same one."

The damp clothes were then produced.

"We're led to believe, from eye-witness accounts, that you were wearing these clothes on Thursday. Correct?"

"Aye, sir."

"Why are they damp then? Did you wash them?"

"Nay, sir. It rained heavily on Thursday an' I got caught in the rain during my milk round. I came home for my dinner as usual an' changed into some dry clothes."

"Mr. Barrett, I want you to have a look at something else." He unfolded the piece of coarse canvas that was heavily stained with dark red-brown patches.

Barrett looked at it and said nothing, nor did he offer any additional information. He yawned again.

"Do you recognize this Barrett?"

"Nay, sir. I don't."

"Are you saying that you've never seen this before?"

"Aye, sir. I've never seen that before."

"Mr. Barrett this was retrieved from your stables, where you work. I cannot imagine that you haven't seen it before."

"Oh, perhaps there wor one like it at the stables," replied Barrett quickly. "I think my mistress; Mrs. Wolfenden gave it to me to keep the horse warm and dry."

"Mr. Barrett, I understand that while you have been here my men asked you to change your clothes. In doing so, they found that the shirt that you removed had blood on it. Is that correct?"

Out of the brown wrapping paper, he produced the bloodstained shirt and placed it in front of Barrett.

"Is this blood, Mr. Barrett?

"It is, sir. The blood is mine. I cut myself shaving the other morning and didn't have time to rinse it off."

"Mr. William Barrett, at this moment in time we have considerable evidence to suspect that John Gill was killed by your hand. As a result, I hereby charge you on suspicion of the wilful murder of one John Gill. You are to be remanded until such time as you are proven innocent."

William Barrett neither looked surprised nor upset. His face was a blank canvas.

Withers turned to the policeman who had brought Barrett from the cells, and who had been present during the short interview.

"Constable, take Mr. Barrett back to his cell."

During their talk, Withers had begun to wonder if the man was insane. The lad had been so badly mutilated he felt only a lunatic could have raped, stabbed, and mutilated a child in such a brutal manner. In light of the behaviour Barrett was displaying, insanity seemed a distinct possibility. He would send Chief Detective-Inspector Dobson and Police Constable Binns over to Keighley, first thing in the morning, to speak to Barrett's mother and other relatives to find out if there was any family history of madness in the family.

Withers had also decided to send some plain-clothed policemen into the community to inquire discretely about Barrett's habits and interests. Having his men in plain clothes would allow them free movement around the community. The real reason behind this move was to find out whether Barratt had a penchant for little boys. Was this something he indulged in? Was he a man who was unable to keep his animal passions in check? Was he as depraved as he thought he had to be considering the heinous nature of the crime and recent stains found on his trousers?

By four o'clock that Saturday afternoon, Barrett was brought up from the Chief Constable's office and found himself before the Borough Justices at the Town Hall on suspicion of having murdered John Gill.

The three borough magistrates on the bench were all present after excusing themselves from family gatherings and other social events planned for the weekend. Magistrates Mr. Arthur Briggs, Mr. John Cass, and Mr. James Burnley listened attentively to the proceedings in an objective manner. It was a special hearing and no one else was in the room, other than the magistrates and a few others directly related to the case.

William Barrett stood in the dock fresh-faced. He was tall, well built, and neatly dressed, but he still looked like the countryman he was. Although he appeared to be listening, he remained detached as if he were just a third party. Despite displaying an air of indifference, he interjected several times to make sure that the exact natures of the circumstances against him were heard. Withers had moved so swiftly that he had not even had time to find a solicitor, and so he stood there unrepresented.

Withers opened the case with his statement.

"The prisoner is charged on suspicion with the wilful murder of a boy named John Gill who was about eight years of age, and was last seen by his mother on Thursday morning at about half-past seven. It would appear from the statement of the mother that this boy has been in the habit of going with the prisoner on his milk rounds very often, and had been very familiar with him.

"On the morning in question the boy was waiting at about 7:30 at his mother's door for the prisoner coming down. The morning was a cold one and his mother told him to come into the house and put his topcoat on. The boy did this, joined the prisoner, got into the milk cart, and this was the last the mother saw of him.

"We shall have evidence to put before Your Worships that this boy was seen at Manningham railway station, where the prisoner had to go for his milk, and was also seen in Queen's Road with him after they left the station. When I took the prisoner into custody this morning he said that the boy had accompanied him to Walmer Villas, Manningham Lane, a spot about two hundred yards from where the boy lived, and that then he left him, saying that he would go home for breakfast.

"Now, Your Worships, I do not wish to put a stronger conclusion on the facts than the evidence warrants. However, I believe the fact is that the prisoner had only one other place to deliver milk after Walmer Villas, and then his journey was at an end, and he would have to go back to the dairy where he was employed in Manningham Lane, within a hundred yards from the murdered boy's house.

"It does seem odd that the boy should leave the prisoner before he had finished his round, and singular to say the boy was never seen to the knowledge of the police, or the parents, or so far as could be ascertained, by anyone else from that time until the dead lad was found.

"The prisoner, having had the boy in his company last of any known person, I felt it my duty from that, and other facts which I have gleaned early this morning, to take him into custody on suspicion. Now I intend calling two witnesses to prove that the boy was seen at Manningham railway station with the prisoner and in Queen's Road, and then, Your Worships, I shall make a statement as to what the prisoner said regarding the boy leaving him at Walmer Villas.

"Now if that was all, Your Worships, I would ask for a remand, but it is not. This man lives at the bottom of

Thorncliffe Road, and last night, as far as my inquiry goes, I found he was working until nearly ten o'clock, about five minutes to ten. Now, to go from this man's home to where the boy lived is hardly a minute's walk, it certainly is not three, and on inquiring of his wife this morning, I found it was twenty-five minutes to eleven before he got home.

"The prisoner has charge of a horse, the stable for which is at the back of Belle Vue, and from that stable to the dairy where the prisoner works is not more than one hundred and fifty yards. I wish to be very cautious in what I say, Your Worships, for I went to that building myself this morning with Sergeant Frank – the door is not locked, and any person can get in.

"However, besides this oddity, the first thing that struck me was that three parts of the stable floor near the top were all wet as if it had been swilled, and under the tap was a can containing clean water. I merely mention that as a suspicious circumstance.

"We had no light, but we struck a few matches, and with the light of these we searched the place but did not find anything at the time. After taking this man into custody, I directed two other officers to go and make a search, which they did. In one part of the stable, they found a sheet of coarse canvas or a stiff wrapper of some sort, which might have been used to cover the body when it was carried to its destination.

"Upon examination of that sheet we were struck by certain marks which Mr. Rimmington, the borough analyst, thought might indicate the presence of blood.

When the sheet was placed before the prisoner he denied all knowledge of it, but afterwards, he made a statement to the effect that he had a sheet of packing something similar given him by his mistress for a horse cover. A further search in the house produced a knife - a very formidable knife.

"There are two wounds upon the body and the knife is about the same dimension of the injuries. When the knife was shown to him, the prisoner denied all knowledge of it at first, but afterwards corrected this statement, stating that his wife had bought a knife somewhere or other of a similar description. The knife has evidently been cleaned, and only recently.

"I will go further and say that this man last night would have to pass within thirty-eight yards of the place where the body was found this morning in going home. In calling at half-past six this morning at the house where the boy resided, he would be within a hundred yards of the spot.

"At 4:35 this morning the policeman on the beat examined the stable where the body was found and can say that at that time it was not there. Knowing all these facts together, I felt justified in arresting the prisoner and bringing him up on suspicion of murder.

"There is a possibility, of course, that the man is innocent, but I think that the circumstantial evidence is so strong that it is necessary for the prisoner to be detained.

"I may mention that the boy has not only been murdered but his body has been mutilated with a savagery which has never been surpassed in this county. I am very sure that the boy was not murdered at the place where his body was found. There are no traces of blood in the Berwick stable, and the limbs that were mutilated do not contain blood to the extent that one would expect to find, even after the lapse of twenty-four hours.

"In fact, the blood seems to have been carefully drawn away from him before the body was cut up. The body was carefully covered over with the boy's clothes. When these were removed, a most shocking sight was disclosed. The parts of the body were tied together with the boy's braces."

Withers went on to give a brief explanation of the place where the remains of the boy were found, the relative positions of the prisoner's house and place of occupation at Belle Vue. He also pointed out that within the half-hour or so that had elapsed between the time of the prisoner calling at Gill's house to inquire if they had heard anything about the missing boy and the discovery of the mutilated remains, there was abundant opportunity for him to go to the stable, return to the yard where the body was found, and then get to the dairy. This was because he would not have to traverse a distance of more than a hundred yards.

He added that according to the opinion of the medical men who had examined the remains, the boy had been dead at least twenty-four hours at the time of the discovery of the remains. He then called evidence for justifying the detention of the prisoner.

To cement his case Withers needed witnesses, including the distraught Mr. and Mrs. Gill, whom it would seem were not allowed to grieve in peace.

Thomas Gill, the strapping, burly cabman, shuffled into the courtroom aided by two constables flanking him on either side and bringing him to his seat. It was awful to see how affected he was, but he was still expected to give testimony in a calm and rational manner. It was asking a lot of a man who less than nine hours ago had seen his son laid out cold on the mortuary slab.

"I've seen the dead body of my son at the mortuary. He wor eight years old. I know the prisoner, an' saw my son in his company." Thomas drew a breath, and before he could continue, William Barrett interrupted.

"He's been with me many a time, has he not?"

"Aye," replied Thomas.

"And since Thursday, I've been to ask about him many times a day," insisted Barrett.

"Aye," agreed Thomas.

"I've asked about him two or three times a day. That is all I know about the boy. He's gone with me many a time."

Mary Ann Gill, who had just come from the mortuary, after insisting that she needed to see for herself that Johnny was dead, was the second eyewitness Withers called. She too had to be helped in and out of the courtroom with two policemen on either side of her. Such was her emotional state that she was given a chair to sit on while on the stand.

She gave her testimony under enormous strain and with deep emotion. Her voice shook from time to time and one had to strain one's ears to hear her. Her mind was still vague from the residue of the opiate and the sheer shock of learning about the death of her son. She struggled to speak or even to think clearly. In between her sobs, she was able to give her testimony, but it was clear to all that she was doing so at a great personal cost. Her answers were slow in coming.

"Deceased wor my son an' would've been eight years of age this February." Mary Ann started to cry. An escaped tendril of hair soon became wrapped around her finger.

"I last saw him alive at twenty minutes past seven last Thursday morning. He wor with the prisoner. I saw him stop, an' my son got into the cart. I've never seen my lad since." The tears flowed, unchecked.

"When did you see the prisoner after that?" asked Withers more gently.

"I saw him several times during the day."

"On Thursday?"

"Aye," she replied in a soft voice.

The magistrates leant forward to hear her response.

"Do you remember what you said to him?"

"Aye." Her voice trembled.

"What did you say the first time you saw him?" Withers was patiently trying to draw out the responses he wanted from her, but poor Mary Ann was just too distraught. However, finally, she replied.

"I first of all sent the girls. An' the boy said he wor out delivering milk."

"When did you see the prisoner yourself?

"It'd be about three o'clock in the afternoon."

"What did you say to him?"

"I asked him if he'd seen the lad an' he said that he'd left him to go to breakfast. He said he wor sliding down the road on the ice." The words were finally coming but her voice betrayed her emotions.

"Did he say where he had left him? Mornington Villas?"

"Walmer Villas, I said," interrupted William Barrett yet again who was clearly following the proceedings closely.

Mary Ann dabbed her eyes with her handkerchief and blew her nose.

"Aye, that's the place," she replied.

"Mrs. Gill, how far is that place from your house?"

"It'd be two hundred yards."

"Did you see the prisoner again?"

"I saw him later at about five o' clock. I asked him if he'd seen him an' he said that he hadn't." Fresh tears started to spill down her cheeks once again.

"Did he say anything further?"

"Nay," she said in a tiny voice.

"Did you make a report to the police?" inquired Withers, knowing that she had.

"We came to the Town Hall late Thursday night."

"Did you see the prisoner again?"

"He came at night an' asked if Johnny had come. There wor a woman present and she said it wor wrong to keep a boy away from his meals for so long."

"Do you remember Friday morning, Mrs. Gill?"

"Aye, he called on Friday morning, but he didn't call during the day."

"Do you remember what he said?"

"Prisoner asked if he'd come and I said that he hadn't. He said nowt more and he went to his work."

"When did he call again?"

"He didn't call till the following morning."

"What time did he call this morning?"

"I'm not sure. My husband saw him."

Finally, Mary Ann's court ordeal was over, but just as Thomas thought that they could go home he was recalled to the witness stand.

"Did you see the prisoner this morning, Mr. Gill?"

"Aye, I think it wor about 6:30."

"What did he say?"

"He said, 'Have you heard anything of John?' That wor all."

"What did you say?"

"I replied that I hadn't an' that I'd been to the Town Hall and the detectives would be looking after him."

"How far is the place where the body was found from your house?"

"Rather better than fifty yards," replied Thomas.

"In going up to work at the dairy, how near would the prisoner go near this passage?"

"He'd go quite close to the end of it."

"Where the body was found?" asked Withers.

"Aye."

"I want you to be particular to the time. Was it about 6:30?"

"Aye, sir. It wor," replied Thomas.

"This man drives a cart, I believe?"

"Aye."

"Do you know where he stables his horse?"

"Somewhere at the back of Belle Vue, I've been told."

At this point, Mr Briggs, one of the magistrates, interjected and addressed the prisoner.

"Do you want to ask any questions of this witness?"

"Nay," replied Barrett. "I've nothing to ask him because he says all that's true about it."

More witnesses followed. Next up was Detective King stating that he had been to the stables to investigate and that he had found the coarse canvas and seen the newly washed floors. He had also been involved in searching Barrett's house and had found the knife in question.

P.C. Kirk explained that the body could not have been placed at the stable during the time of his beat because he had stood directly on the spot where the body was found, and there was nothing there right up until his last inspection at just after 4:30 a.m.

Joseph Bucke had rallied enough to give evidence stating how it was that he had found the body and how he had fetched Albert Teale and then finally found the constable on duty and brought him back to the stables.

Mrs. Hannah Wolfenden gave evidence next.

"Mrs. Wolfenden, did you give the prisoner this cloth?" asked Withers holding up the stained piece of canvas.

"Nay, sir, I did not. However, I have used a similar cloth to cover one of the machines in the dairy."

At this point Barrett interjected once again.

"Mistress, the canvas came from the dairy, I think Mrs. Beaton must've given it to me. I'm sure she told me that this wor cloth left over from the dairy that'd been used for another purpose."

She was asked one or two further questions before stepping down.

Finally, Mr. Rimmington presented his evidence. He stated that it was too early to say whether the stains on the canvas were blood and that further investigation and analysis were necessary.

"We have heard the evidence this afternoon regarding this difficult case," stated Mr. Briggs the magistrate, "and it is sufficient to remand the prisoner in custody until Wednesday. Mr. Barrett, if you need to consult with your friends on this matter, you may do so. The policemen will assist you in this matter."

The first person Barrett saw inside his cell that Saturday evening was his boss, Mr. Wolfenden. Wolfenden was very upset that people were accusing Barrett of such a heinous crime and insisted on paying for his defence. He assured Barrett that he knew a good lawyer, one of the best, in the form of John Whipp Craven, and promised that he would go with haste to Keighley himself to engage his services.

The second visitor was Margaret Barrett, minus baby Nellie. She arrived and departed composed and brimming with confidence, telling reporters, who were milling around Town Hall, that this was all a misunderstanding. Her husband would be released shortly and the real killer would soon be apprehended, as the police had no evidence to connect her Willie to the crime.

Willie Barrett's first night in his cell was very festive. He spent most of it chatting with the constables on duty. Occasionally he would break out into song during the night, crooning in a voice that no one would have labelled melodious.

In light of the severity of the crime, one could not deny that his behaviour was indeed, all rather odd.

CHAPTER FOUR – SUNDAY 30TH DECEMBER 1888

Sunday Schools within Manningham and beyond on Sunday were empty. People had either read about, or heard about, the murder of John Gill and mothers were keeping their children indoors and off the streets. Gossip was rife, and there was a great air of excitement that the very villain that had ripped up the women in the East End of London was now prowling the streets of Bradford. Some mothers had already decided that they would not be sending their children back to school until the killer was safely behind bars.

People with a sense of morbid curiosity came in their droves on the first weekend after the murder. The scene of the crime where 'Jack the Ripper' had been, and which was still being worked by the policeforce, had become an overnight sensation. Crowds were so large that extra policemen had to work overtime to contain and refrain them from getting too close. After being dispersed there, they went on to the house of the Gill family, where blinds were now drawn, mirrors hastily draped in black, and where a family was trying to mourn the tragic loss of their beloved child in private.

Despite the house seemingly being shut off from the outside world, it had not prevented people standing around in small groups hovering in order to get a glimpse of the affected family. Others just stood around and nattered, feeding off the latest gossip or titbit that they had heard. One slatternly woman, arms akimbo, loudly voiced her bigoted opinion outside the house, while some in the crowd nodded in agreement as she spoke.

"I'm telling you now, it's the work of them filthy Jews 'ere in Bradford. One of 'em has done this. We all know it's Jews tha' like to kill our Christian bairns come Christmas."

A constable, who had been standing on the fringe of the crowd, heard her and moved her along before she could make any more inciting and hateful anti-Semitic comments.

It wasn't long before local news reporters and scouts began hounding people connected to the case to give their account of what had happened. Some who were approached relished the opportunity of being a voice to be heard. Others, like the Gills, really just wanted to be left alone to grieve in peace. But the death of their child had not been a natural one and the murder had attracted a great deal of attention.

The Bradford Observer had been particularly busy sending out their scouts that day, and one of them was now interviewing Thomas in his front room. Tom felt numb. He did not want to speak to the reporter, but he hoped that by doing so, someone would come forward with some information that would add to the case. This was the only reason for granting the interview.

He spoke in a flat voice devoid of emotion as he recounted his side of the story. The young reporter, no more than twenty, sat perched on the edge of a chair in the darkened drawing room. He listened intently, notebook on his knees, pencil in hand, writing it all down in shorthand while Thomas spoke.

"My boy wor, I believe, a great favourite with the milkman. The milkman, however, has not been here very long, an' I never heard my boy speak specially about him. He always wished to get up in the morning to join the milk cart.

"He wor a very feeling lad and wor liked by everybody. Today his teachers at the Sunday school have been up asking particular as to the case.

"Johnny wor a good lad. He never stopped away from home, an' hence our alarm an' concern on Thursday an' Friday. My son attended school both on Sundays and weekdays with regularity. He wor at school up to the Christmas holidays. He wor a very careful lad an' wor pleased that he'd have some money that he'd saved to put in the bank at the close of the holidays.

"I saw the body at the mortuary an' kissed my poor boy's cold, wet lips. My wife saw the body yesterday; she had to go an' see it. It wor his face only we saw; a sweet face, quite placid an' bonnie. If they'd brought home my child drowned, I imagine I could've borne the loss with more fortitude, but the very thought of this awful an' terrible mutilation an' butchery has completely overwhelmed me an' rendered me quite unfit for anything.

"The affair wor a terrible shock to us. It will, I fear, be the death of my wife. We get no sleep. My wife doesn't yet know the awful character of the mutilations. We really daren't tell her, she is so bad. It's simply terrible. We're quite overcome. This is really awful to me to think of. I cannot understand how such a deed could've been done, for as I've said, Johnny wor liked by everybody."

The last few sentences were spoken with difficulty, his voice breaking as he spoke.

James Withers did not take the weekend off and demanded that his constables do the same. They had work to be done, and so instead of spending quality time with friends and family, they were back at the Belle Vue stables looking for anything that they might have missed the day before. This time they came well prepared with their Bullseye lanterns to shine into any dark corners.

"Right, gentlemen, I don't have to tell you that this is an important case, and I want to make sure that whoever did this does not walk free. Unfortunately, at this stage we don't have too much to go on. Therefore, it's important that we find as much evidence as possible to link it to the killer. We'll divide this stable into quarters and we'll search it methodically. Once we've finished a quarter, we'll move on to the next. Any questions?"

Every inch of the stable was examined from top to bottom, making sure that no stone was left unturned, as was Withers' motto. It was not long before their persistence paid off.

"Sir, we've found something."

One of his men presented Withers with a hammer that they had just retrieved from the roof space.

"Good man!" exclaimed Withers. "Can you shine more light on it for me?"

The officer held his Bullseye a little closer and Withers leant in to get a closer look. He was excited to see that there were some brown stains on the tool, possibly bloodstains.

After another hour or so of searching, they found their most promising piece of evidence yet. Underneath a pile of straw, carefully hidden away, were three damp cloths that looked as if there were still traces of blood present on the edges.

Chief Constable Withers was now very animated. When looking at the cloths he was of the opinion that these were probably the cloths used to clean the body after death that Doctor Lodge had mentioned. However, the pink tinges found around the edges were very faint, and there was no doubt that these too had been well washed and thoroughly rinsed. Despite this, he hoped Rimmington would be able to find enough evidence to say unequivocally that the stains were indeed blood, and that he could then link the cloths back to Barrett.

Despite the findings this morning, Withers was fast becoming frustrated with this case. He knew that even if they did find evidence of blood on both the hammer and the damp cloths, it still did not tie Barrett to the murder. This was largely due to some disturbing information he had recently learned.

The stable key that was normally in Barrett's possession had been missing for over a week. The stables that were usually locked, with Barrett the possessor of the key, had not been locked during the time of the murder. This meant that the stables could have been accessed and used by anybody.

He was also acutely aware that a case of this magnitude could tarnish or even destroy his career if he did not solve it and get a conviction.

CHAPTER FIVE – MONDAY 31ST DECEMBER 1888

Withers, frustrated by not finding anything else, decided that the next logical step would be to open up the drains to the stable. Large amounts of water were used to flush the pipes clean, but he was still hoping that they would be able to recover some evidence.

Working the floor of the stable was laboriously slow. Each detective grovelled on his hands and knees, carefully removing and collecting the dirt between each and every flagstone. Once they had removed the dirt, they took up the flagstones one by one and searched the drains beneath them. They were looking for anything: blood, hair, even the tiniest of bone fragments. They also removed the granular deposits from the sink in the hopes of finding further evidence. But despite their diligence, nothing that was obvious was found.

During the morning they also examined the lock to the coach house, knowing that the key had been reported missing. Surprisingly, what they retrieved from inside the escutcheon was part of a broken key.

Later that morning, the case soon took another blow. Withers learned that the stables had previously been rented out to a butcher. The situation was lurching from bad to worse.

The only evidence Withers knew that he had against Barrett was an armful of circumstantial evidence that was mounting by the hour. But he wondered, without any hard physical evidence other than what they had, whether it would be enough.

After examining the Belle Vue Stables, Withers then sent his men over to the Ashfield Dairy to see if they could find anything there, and they did. They found a hatchet hidden in a coalhole. The hatchet was stained; brown stains that definitely looked like blood.

James Withers was beginning to feel more confident.

John Whipp Craven, Barrett's lawyer from Weatherhead & Burr, was a most eligible bachelor. Every matron in the village of Keighley and beyond had their eye on him as a potential suitor for their spinster daughters. Although relatively new as a solicitor, and having only been appointed four years prior, what he lacked in experience he made up for in tenacity and energy within the courtroom. Some more churlish called his performances 'theatrical.' But few could deny that he was a very able lawyer with a string of successful defence trials already achieved.

And it was not surprising. He came from a family of lawyers. His father, Joseph Craven, was one of the oldest magistrates still sitting on the bench in Keighley. He didn't have to go too far for an ear when seeking advice on how to handle a complicated case.

Craven's best asset was that he was an opportunist who seized a moment and cleverly manipulated events to suit the situation. He was also a master at seducing and working the media. He had a love-hate relationship with reporters and journalists, whom he viewed as a fickle lot, and dallied with them when he didn't want them to know too much. When reporters congratulated themselves for finally getting a story out of him when he did acquiesce to be interviewed, he was merely using them to his advantage. He was merely making sure that his voice was heard so as to sway the populace and, hopefully, the jury of the day.

Today would be no different. He was actually looking forward to being interviewed by the hungry reporters that he knew would be circling on Monday afternoon after Mr. James Gwynne Hutchinson's brief and closed Coroner's Inquest.

Sensationalism of any kind sells tabloids and newspapers, and readers of the John Gill case seemed insatiable. It was not only due to its grisly and gruesome content, but gossip mongers continued to spread the story that the dastardly deed was the work of Jack the Ripper. As a result, Bradford had been invaded by reporters from all over the country, each trying to get the latest news, to be the first to publish a story that no one else had read, or from an angle that no one else had thought of. And to get this news they clambered to interview people close to the case.

John Whipp Craven now emerged from Town Hall, his black robes flowing behind him as he battled a stiff breeze coming off the moors. He purposefully ignored the impatient reporters who had immediately pounced on him, hungry for news. Instead, he forged ahead. And then he hesitated, turned, and walked back to the group of eager men. His smile did not meet his eyes.

"Gentlemen, rest assured that my client, William Barrett, is innocent. My client is able to account for his movements on Thursday, Friday, and Saturday until his arrest. Every minute of every hour, from the time the lad left him, until my client's apprehension, is known.

"Of course, a lot of what he's said can only be corroborated by his wife, and who is debarred from giving evidence due to their relationship. But I've no doubt that we'll be able to prove his innocence beyond doubt even without her assistance.

"Mr. Barrett denies, in the strongest manner possible, that he had anything at all to do with this murder, and he's certain that his innocence will be fully established.

"He asserts that the lad left him at half-past eight on Thursday morning, just as he was about to deliver milk at 9 Walmer Villas, saying that he'd run home for his breakfast, and promising, as he went away, that he'd come back and join the prisoner on his long milk round, as he was frequently in the habit of doing for the sake of the ride. The prisoner went directly to the dairy after finishing his round, and there's evidence to show that he got there at the usual time, about nine o' clock, and after taking the horse out of the cart and leading it up to the stable, went on his late morning's milk round with a hand-cart because the roads were slippery.

"We are very confident that this case will be dismissed very shortly for lack of evidence."

With that, he flashed them a smile and disappeared into a waiting cab.

Chief Constable Withers did not share Craven's view of the prisoner's innocence, and this was especially so after he heard from his men that Barrett continued to display unusual behaviour. Withers also felt that Barrett was developing an unnatural growing confidence that he would soon be exonerated.

One had to wonder why, thought Withers. *Was he feeble of mind that he didn't quite appreciate just how much trouble he was in?*

When Withers had interviewed Wolfenden earlier on that afternoon, he had been told that Barrett was a man of excellent character. He wasn't addicted to drink, nor did he profane much. Wolfenden was so convinced that Barrett could not possibly have committed this monstrous crime that he told Withers that he had personally engaged John Craven to defend his employee and would be paying for his defence.

Withers wondered when hearing this if Wolfenden had considered just how long the case could drag on for, or how much it would cost. He wondered too why an employer would go to so much trouble and personal cost for his hired help.

Was Barrett's behaviour then that of a man who had a clear conscience and who felt that at any minute now he would be released because he was entirely innocent? Was that it? Or was

Barrett confident because he was a manipulative, unscrupulous man who knew that every possible connection between himself and the crime had been thoroughly and systematically removed?

That he knew that he had cleaned everything, from the knife to the clothes, to the cloths, to the stables. That the drains had been thoroughly swilled, the stable scrubbed, and the crime scene devoid of any evidence. That the murder was committed in a place where any flesh or blood discovered would be in dispute because the stable had previously been tenanted to a butcher. That the crime had occurred in a stable with no key and open to anyone. That doubt would arise because outwardly he was a charming man who lived a seemingly exemplary, ordinary life of a newly married, family man. That he knew that the dreadful deed had been carried out in a calculated, methodical and well-planned manner; faultlessly executed.

Was Barrett confident because he knew that he was already several steps ahead of everyone else?

Deep down James Withers had the feeling that the case he had started building against Barrett was slowly disintegrating like a sandcastle built upon an incoming tide.

That evening a letter arrived addressed to the editor of a local newspaper, in the hopes that it would be published in the morning. It read:

'The atrocity in Manningham has not been committed by Barrett, but by the real Whitechapel murderer.

'On Friday night, as I was passing the Standard Hotel, I saw a man who was twice brought up at Leman Street for the Whitechapel murder. I was in London at the time, and that man's face made a very unfavourable impression on my mind.

'Hoping this will put the police on the look out.'

On New Year's Day there were no family celebrations for Felix Rimmington or Samuel Lodge. Instead, both men were working diligently on the case.

Felix Rimmington had spent several days carefully sifting through the fine debris that the police had collected from the drains, the sink, and the floor of the Wolfenden stable.

His examinations were painstakingly slow only because he wanted to do a thorough job and not rush the results. Withers had been putting pressure on him to give him a decisive answer as to whether any of the items that had been recovered to date had blood on them. Withers would have to wait a little longer before he got his answer. Rimmington had an inkling that it would not be the answer he was looking for.

He knew Withers would be disappointed when he heard the results of the canvas examination. He had tested the material for blood but had found none. When he had received it, it was wet, very wet, and nothing could be found. However, when examining the canvas with a magnifying glass he was able to lift and examine a small number of fine fair hairs that were definitely of interest.

With the aid of a high-powered microscope, he was expecting to see the hair cut at an angle, as one would expect to see if the hair had been human and cut by a barber. They were not. They were tapered to a point at the end.

This is not human hair, thought Rimmington, *more like that from the back of an animal.*

James Withers was not the only one who was disappointed with the results.

For Doctor Samuel Lodge it was going to be a particularly busy day. He had three doctors from two different parties scheduled to visit the mortuary today, two of whom were coming to do an independent examination.

The first two learned gentlemen to arrive at the mortuary that morning were Doctor Hime from Bradford, and Doctor Roberts from Keighley. They had been retained by the defence team to do the independent study.

John Craven had wanted an independent autopsy to determine the cause of death. Although Doctor Lodge had no objections, he did feel that the request was rather ludicrous, considering that there were no arguments that death had occurred by stabbing. In any event, the cause of death had no bearing on the case. However, he would indulge Craven's wishes.

Doctor Thomas Whiteside Hime was an exceptionally gifted man with great powers of observation. He had given several lectures of late on the theory of germs, trying to convince his colleagues that germs were a big problem and that they were the cause of many diseases. Some of his colleagues were still rather sceptical, but they did find his work on wool sorter's disease and anthrax far more interesting and plausible. Thus, he managed to hang on to his reputation.

Doctor Lodge invited the doctors into his mortuary and relayed to the men what he had found during his investigation, as well as to the cause of death. He then proceeded to update them on his latest findings, saying that on further investigation he had now found one of the lungs inside the stomach, along with the ears that were first thought to be missing. He said that he had discovered that the liver had been sliced from the body and then replaced. On examination, the replaced liver hardly looked like a liver at all, as it had been dried out in some way. He had recovered all the body parts that were first thought to be missing, except for the anus and penis.

The two stab wounds to the left breast of the child had been done in such a forceful manner that they, to quote Lodge directly, 'would have stopped an elephant.' The force of the stabbing had not only penetrated muscle but had also smashed through the bones.

On examining the clothes, he found that they were all accounted for. When he examined the trousers, they were soiled, indicating that the boy was still wearing these before he had been killed. The soiled pair of trousers was also indicative that the child had experienced a terrible fright during the last moments of his life. Inside the digestive system, he had found evidence of undigested pieces of spiced currant cake.

After several hours, the visiting doctors concluded their independent investigation. They agreed with Doctor

Lodge on all his findings, except one. They differed on the cause of death.

Where Doctor Lodge had opined that death was caused by two stab wounds to the heart, Doctor Hime concluded that the knife had missed all the major arteries; one wound being above the heart and the second, below the heart. He therefore doubted that this was the cause of death although he was reluctant to say exactly how the child had died without making further investigations.

Thanking Lodge for accommodating him, Doctor Hime then left the mortuary to seek out Doctor Ridley. John Craven had hired both of them to interview William Barrett to establish his sanity. This was in retaliation to the inquiry made by Withers some days prior, when he had sent his men over to Kildwick to establish whether there had been any madness in the family. He had been disappointed on being told that there was none. John Craven, however, now wanted to get an expert opinion on the matter to dispel any further slur on his client's state of mind.

It did not take Doctors Hime and Ridley too long before they were able to say that the prisoner seemed calm and lucid, leaving the impression that they thought that he was perfectly rational and totally sane.

Doctor Lodge had one more visitor that day, a Doctor Phillips, who had travelled all the way up from London.

He was the divisional surgeon from Whitechapel where equally hideous murders had taken place of late involving several prostitutes. He had come to Bradford, at the request of Chief Constable James Withers, to find out if the murder of John Gill could be linked in any way to the murders in London done by the hand of Jack the Ripper.

There were several reasons for this request. Withers had received several letters urging him to look into the possibility. There was also the Cahill incident that he had publically dismissed as a family prank. However, no suspect had been found and he did not want a town in panic. Calling on an expert opinion in this matter seemed prudent.

Doctor Phillips inspected the body at the mortuary at length and remained in consultation with Samuel Lodge for several hours. The Metropolitan surgeon finally concluded that it was his expert opinion that Johnny Gill had not been killed by the same hand as those who had died in the East End of London.

Concerning the mutilation of the genital area, however, he agreed with the local doctors; that the boy had probably been raped before or after death.

Later that morning Barrett was brought up on remand before the Bradford Borough Court. It was the third time he had come up before the magistrates, and for the first time, the court would now be open to a public hearing. The news attracted great excitement and large crowds.

The atmosphere outside the courts was almost carnival-like. Street entertainers came to make an extra penny or two with a juggling act, four musicians, a dancing bear, and an organ grinder. Other opportunists arrived early to set up their stalls in Town Hall Square and to take advantage of the milling crowds. Men and women jostled for position to be one of the first to be allowed into the courtroom, growing more impatient with each passing minute. They had gathered well before the doors were even likely to open, just to ensure a seat.

The Bradford Murder, as it was now publically called, had dominated conversations at dinner parties of the rich, to gatherings around kitchen tables of the poor. People had discussed the case as if they had been there, each one an expert on who was guilty of the crime. Some swore that it was the work of Jack the Ripper and that Barrett was innocent. Others, from opposing camps, had already gathered with their placards proclaiming Barrett a monster and were baying for his blood.

Withers looked out of his office window and was appalled at the unruly crowd. He was concerned that he would soon have a riot on his hands between the two factions if he did not act fast. He decided there and then that the best way forward was to open the court doors an hour earlier and allow people early access. Due to the nature of the crime, however, he also felt that it was too delicate a matter for women's ears and those of the youth.

When this was publically announced a few minutes later, cheer and jeers simultaneously erupted. The women were furious. The men, however, were elated, for the ruling meant that more of them would now find seats.

As soon as the doors were flung open a wave of humanity surged forward, causing a bottleneck as they all tried to fit through the doors at once. Within a few minutes, certainly no more than three, all the seats were occupied and men were being turned away. Special seating had been reserved for a large number of news reporters who had come from far and wide to report on this sensational case, and these too were now fully occupied. The courtroom was packed. There was not a spare seat to be had, either in the lower or upper gallery.

A hush fell over the room as William Barrett was brought up. He walked towards the dock in an overt public display of nonchalance; one hand thrust deep into his trouser pocket, a swagger to his walk. However, despite the bravado, to the more observant eye, the last few days in the cells had taken their toll. His eyes appeared heavy. Dark rings accompanied them. Men strained their necks to get a better view of him as he climbed the few steps to stand in the dock and curled his hands tightly around the rail in front of him. He stood facing Mr. J. R. Armitage and nine other magistrates on the Bench.

Concerning the legal teams, Mr. Craven was representing the prisoner, Mr. James Freeman was representing the family, and Chief Constable Withers was there to represent the police.

Mr. Withers stood up and started to give an outline of the evidence to date. He stroked his bushy walrus moustache with his thumb and index finger several times during his delivery, almost as if he were trying to tame it. James Withers came across as confident. His speech delivery was steady and measured, and several times at significant moments, he paused and fixed his rheumy eyes on Barrett. Occasionally Barrett swept his eyes over Withers with an air of indifference, and from time to time, he leaned casually on the dock rail, but still took everything in.

"Gentlemen of the court, I will prove today that the deceased was seen in the prisoner's company sometime after the hour at which the prisoner said the boy went home to breakfast. In fact, I have witnesses willing to swear that they saw the boy up to two hours later in the prisoner's company, which will show that the prisoner lied in the statement he made about the time the boy left him.

"Evidence will also be forthcoming to show that a light was seen in the prisoner's stable much later than usual on Thursday night.

"On Friday it will be proved that after Mrs. Gill made to him the remark about detectives being on his track, that very night the stable was lit up at eleven o'clock - a most unusual thing.

"You will hear from the matron of the Servants' Home, who will state that she was awakened in the middle of the night by a sound of scraping and swilling in the stable and from a servant in the same establishment who will tell you that the stable was lit up much earlier than usual the following morning.

"Nellie Pearson, a single woman, will finally tell you that a few minutes before ten on Thursday morning, when according to the prisoner's statement the boy had gone home to breakfast, the deceased had actually delivered milk to her house, on behalf of Barrett.

"Another woman on the prisoner's milk round will attest to the fact that when she received her milk from him at around eleven o'clock the prisoner smelt of drink and was agitated.

"You will also hear that the prisoner left home Friday morning at half-past five, long before he was due at work, and was seen by a young girl who lived next door to him and saw him going towards Belle Vue Stables.

"I have another witness who will tell you that there was a light on in the stables on Saturday morning, far earlier than usual. Finally, you will hear from the father of the deceased, Thomas Gill, who'll tell you that on Saturday morning the prisoner knocked on his door, but approached not from the left as one would expect coming from his home, but from the right-hand side. Quite possibly coming from Back Mellor Street where the deceased was left.

"Mr. Rimmington, the borough analyst, has now tested the three wet cloths that were found concealed under some hay in the stables last Sunday. He has confirmed that although they were well washed, he was still able to determine that they contained traces of blood. The analysis of the other evidence retrieved has not yet been completed.

"As to the motive of the crime, it is singular that the part of the body that would have been evidence against any man having committed an unnatural crime - was missing."

Withers paused, cleared his throat and fixed his eyes on Barrett. He continued. "In conclusion, when the prisoner's clothing was taken from him there were certain marks found upon it. The prisoner was certainly of strong animal passions and not able to govern himself within the bounds of decency!" Once again, Withers focused on Barrett.

Barrett did not flinch at the insinuation and held his gaze.

One by one, Withers called his witnesses to show that Barrett had lied in his statement. Both Thomas and Mary Ann were again called to take the stand and both of them were still very much affected by the events.

Thomas was the first witness to be called, and this time, he was able to tell the court that on the Saturday morning, Barrett had knocked on the door coming from the direction of the stable.

Mary Ann was called next. She walked stiffly into the courtroom, looking a little unkempt and much older than her current age. She was haggard and gaunt, her skin translucently pale and stretched tight over her cheekbones. Her eyes were dull and her hair no longer in its usual neat bun. When she spoke, her voice was flat. It was clear that she would need a seat yet again, and this was duly provided.

She relayed all that had happened in a mechanical way, but this time she did not cry. Her tear ducts had dried up, her emotions a wasteland.

Alice Beal, fast approaching thirty, had a physique that foretold her occupation. She took the stand.

"Please state your name, address and occupation," said Withers.

"My name is Alice Beal. I live at 10 Walmer Villas. I'm the cook for Mr. Samuel Hemmingway."

Samuel Hemmingway, a dry soap manufacturer, and his wife Emma had several children, many of whom were still living at home. They lived directly opposite number 9 in this well-to-do, fashionable street.

"I saw the prisoner an' the boy together on Thursday last at about half-past eight. I watched the prisoner deliver milk to both number nine an' number thirteen Walmer Villas. While I wor looking at the milk being delivered I noticed that a little lad wor standing in the cart."

"And who was this little lad, Miss. Beal?"

"It wor Johnny Gill, sir," replied Annie.

"And how do you know that it was young Gill?"

"I visited the mortuary an' the dead lad wor the same one that I saw standing in the cart."

Next on the stand was Nellie Pearson who lived at 15 Bertram Road.

"On the Wednesday night I'd slept at Birkenshaw. The following morning, on Thursday, I returned to Bradford, arriving at about twenty minutes or twenty-five minutes past nine. From the train station, I walked to catch a tram from the top of Darley Street and from there I took the tram to the bottom of St. Paul's Road. I got off there and then walked the rest of the way home. After a ten-minute walk, I arrived home at about ten minutes to ten.

"I was just taking off my jacket when there was a knock on the door. I opened it and there was a little boy delivering my milk. The lad had delivered milk to my door before on two previous occasions, so I immediately recognized him. The milkman, William Barrett, was standing next to the cart that was right in front of my garden gate - a distance no more than five yards.

"I've known the prisoner for some four or five weeks now and have taken milk from him nearly every morning during that period.

"I saw the body at the mortuary and I was able to identify him as being the lad at my front door. Unfortunately, I cannot say exactly the type of clothing he was wearing although I do remember them as being dark in colour."

Court then adjourned for lunch.

After the court had resumed, young Bertha Pickard, not quite 13 and still living with her parents at sixteen Church Street, took the stand.

"On Thursday last, at about ten o' clock, I saw the prisoner call into Bertram Road with his cart and horse but didn't see anyone else with him. I know the prisoner well as he has called with the milk in the neighbourhood of Bertram Road many times now and I could see the gates at the back of the houses from my window.

"However, I couldn't see from my house anyone delivering milk at the back door of the house occupied by the Hamilton family outside, which was where the prisoner had stopped."

Mr. Freeman, solicitor for the Gills, at that moment interjected stating that he would like to point out to the court that the distance between the house in Bertram Road and the house in Church Street was a mere four or a five-minute walk.

"It is not important whether Miss. Pickard could or could not see the boy with the milkman. What is important with this witness is that it establishes a timeline in relation to the other witnesses," he explained.

Next on the stand was Elizabeth Cragg, wife of Thomas Cragg, a coachman from 22 Bishop Street. She said that she knew the prisoner.

"On Thursday, 27th December the prisoner 'ad come at about 10:45 a.m. to the 'ouse with the milk. 'E wor in a great 'urry an' smelt a little of drink although 'e didn't look any the worse for it. I excused 'im because it wor Christmas time."

"Mrs. Cragg, can you tell us more about the alcohol you detected on the prisoner?"

"Well, the smell of the alcohol was right strong an' to me it smelled like 'e 'ad been drinking rum. However, the prisoner seemed rather agitated an' looked a little cross. As 'e seemed to be in rather a 'urry and as I wor in a 'urry myself, I didn't stop to talk to 'im."

Mr. Craven, who had been unusually quiet during these witness testimonies, decided to recall Benjamin Abbot.

"Mr. Abbot, are you sure about the time you saw a light on in the stable?"

"Quite sure, sir."

"And what makes you so sure?"

"Well, I had just finished sewing several sets of curtains when I took out my pocket watch and noted the time. It was ten thirty-five. I then packed the curtains into their boxes, locked up the store, and started walking home. It would not have taken me more than ten minutes by the time I passed the stable."

"You are certain too when you saw the light, Mr. Abbot? On Friday was it?"

"Quite certain," Abbot replied. "But on the previous occasion I am not certain whether it was a Wednesday or a Thursday night. I should not like to say."

There were several other witnesses, including the matron from the Servants' Home, who stated that she had heard strange noises coming from the stable for about 20 minutes that had frightened her.

Craven cross-examined this witness too.

"Mrs. Kendall, you say that you heard a noise supposedly coming from the stables on Friday night.

"Have you decided what sort of noise you heard that frightened you so?" Craven asked with a hint of sarcasm in his voice.

"I don't know what sort of noise it wor, sir. Only that it wor summat I'd never heard before. An' it did frighten me because it wor so unusual."

"Come now, Mrs. Kendall. A woman of your age? Frightened, while you were safely tucked up in bed?"

People laughed. Mrs. Kendall blushed.

"Could the noise you heard have been from workmen in the area?"

"Nay, sir, the noise wor definitely coming from the stable. It wor a sawing or a swishing noise."

"A sound like someone was throwing ash onto a road?"

"Possibly, aye."

"So, Mrs. Kendall, if I told you that around the time that you thought you heard a noise coming from the stable, workmen were in your area throwing ash down on the road. Could it be now that this was what you heard?"

"Possibly, sir."

"Thank you, Mrs. Kendall. No more questions. You may step down."

Withers was disappointed at how easily Eliza Kendall had been persuaded to change her statement.

Police Constable William Henry Firth was next on the stand. He said, "On Saturday morning I received the prisoner into custody at nine twenty from the Chief Constable and conveyed him to Town Hall. He made a statement about the boy.

He said:

'Johnny came to my cart at 7:20 on Thursday morning in Thorncliffe Road. He remained with the cart until I had

breakfast. He then went with me to Manningham Railway Station for the milk. When I had the milk, I proceeded up Queens Road to Walmer Villas. I delivered milk at No. 9 Walmer Villas, and Johnny said that he would go and get his breakfast. I said all right, and then delivered my milk at No. 13 Walmer Villas and went to the dairy.'

"I searched the prisoner the same morning at Town Hall and found the property, now produced, on the prisoner. The property consisted of a scarf, three milk books, a pipe, envelope, watch and key, purse, three shillings and five pence in money, tobacco, a piece of lead pencil, and a handkerchief. The clothing produced is that worn by the prisoner at the time of the arrest.

"I was in charge of the prisoner at 11:40 the same morning. At the time, he had not been charged with any offence. The prisoner then made another statement.

He said:

'The sister to John Gill has been with me to the station several times for milk but having read about outrages on girls I had sent her away from the cart many times.'

"That is all, Your Worship."

Detective Sergeant Abbey then produced the shirt that Barrett was wearing on the day young Gill went missing, which had certain marks on it that were cause for suspicion.

Detective King said that he had found a bread knife at the prisoner's house that had been newly cleaned and at the stable a piece of packing canvas. He then went on to tell the court that Barrett had first denied knowing anything about the knife when he had been interviewed at

Town Hall. It was at this point that John Craven interrupted him.

"Your Worships, I would like to point out that when my client made these statements they were made while he was in custody, and therefore, no statement made by him at that time should be submitted as evidence."

James Withers was like a bulldog all over a bone. He was on his feet immediately. "Your Worships, Mr. Barrett was not in custody at that time, he was simply being… detained."

Laughter rippled throughout the court.

After some minutes of internal arguing on what should or should not be admissible, the two men finally had their answer from Mr. Armitage.

"Gentlemen, we have decided that the evidence given by the prisoner while he was in custody will be inadmissible."

John Craven smiled in triumph. Withers scowled.

Detective King was able to continue. "We also found in the stable a piece of coarse harden or canvas and pieces of rag, all of which were stained. A hammer was likewise discovered and on Monday, we found a hatchet in Wolfenden's coalhole. The floor to the stable was wet when the police entered it and the pieces of rag etcetera, have all been handed over to Mr. Rimmington, the borough analyst."

Mr. Rimmington was the last witness to be called to the stand.

"Mr. Rimmington, have you had time to examine the items sent to your laboratory?" asked Withers.

"Not all, but I have been able to examine some items."

"Could you please tell the court what you have examined to date and the results?"

"I was able to determine that there was no blood on the canvas that was produced. I did find some fine hairs of interest, but on further examination, they proved to be animal and not human hairs.

"With regards to the three rags that were found in the stable I can say that despite the fact that each had been well-washed I was able to determine coagulate material on one of them."

"By coagulate material do you mean blood, Mr. Rimmington?" asked Withers to clarify.

"That is correct, Mr. Withers."

"Have you examined anything else?"

"Not as yet."

After listening to the mounting evidence against him Barrett's initial apparent indifference during the morning had given way to an air of keen interest. For the remainder of the day he followed the evidence with the closest of attention. He stood in the dock and looked over at Craven, his face etched with grave concern.

Withers stood up again. "Your Worships, this was our last witness. We would like to adjourn until next Wednesday."

Craven sprang up at once and objected strongly. "Your Worships, this is preposterous! Another week? My client needs to have this case moved on as quickly as possible."

Withers was quick to retort.

"Your Worships, due to the severity of this crime, and because we are still gathering evidence, it is necessary that we are given this time to complete our investigations. I also need to consult with the Treasury due to the magnitude of this case."

Armitage paused for a few seconds. The filled courtroom was silent.

Suddenly the silence was broken as the gavel struck the wood. "Court will adjourn for another week," replied Armitage.

This time Craven scowled. As he stood up to leave, Withers turned towards him and on making eye contact, smiled triumphantly. Craven responded with a thunderous black look, turned on his heels, and left the room.

CHAPTER SEVEN - THURSDAY 3RD JANUARY 1889

When reporters heard that Mr. John Procter Wolfenden was putting up the money for Barrett's defence, they decided that there had to be a story there somewhere. After all, this was a most unusual and generous gesture of any employer. One determined reporter had beaten the rest of his colleagues to an interview by tracking Wolfenden to his home before work hours.

When approached for an interview Wolfenden readily agreed. He told the reporter that he was very keen to help young Barrett out in any way he could. What he did, however, and with calculating deliberateness, was to publically mock Withers, his constabulary, and the evidence presented so far through the power of the media.

When Withers saw the published interview in a local paper that evening his pasty face, usually devoid of colour, was puce with rage.

"Confound this man!" he exclaimed to Dobson who had just walked into his office. He thumped his fist onto the table for emphasis, rattling the teacup, with the overflow ending up sloshing around in the saucer.

"How dare this man air his opinion so readily like this while the case is in progress? He has painted Barrett in such glowing terms that he could soon be the new saint of Bradford! Not only that, after the jurors read this rubbish, for no doubt they will, the damage will already have been done! I've also heard that he's telling people that Barrett couldn't be the murderer because someone who had medical knowledge did the mutilations. The audacity of this man! It shouldn't be allowed, Dobson! It shouldn't be allowed!"

Dobson picked up the newspaper and started reading the offending article.

'Speaking of the sad affair, in general, terms, so far as I can see at present I do not think that the police authorities can bring anything against Barrett.

'I have always looked on him as a respectable, industrious man. He was very attentive to his duties. And before being married, he lived in the house with us at the farm at Cross Hills in Kildwick. I believe I never had a more agreeable and respectable man staying in my house. He never took a beer, and invariably conducted himself in a most becoming way.

'After Barrett got married he worked a short time for another party, but when I opened this dairy, as he was a good trustworthy servant, I employed him again.

'The harden wrapper, or coarse canvas, which the police found and are having analysed in the hopes of finding traces of blood on it, was bought for an engine cover. Barrett asked if he might take it to the stables to cover the horse and he got permission to do so. This was about two months ago. The police found the canvas in the stable and noticed some marks on it. My opinion is, and I have some experience in such matters, that the marks were only similar to marks naturally to be found on covers lying in a stable.

'The urine of a horse, with which a cover not infrequently gets saturated, would naturally leave a red or brownish impression. I'm sanguine that the effort to trace blood on the cover will fail.

'As to the story that the body was found in a bag, that is a mistake; for there can be no question that the body was wrapped up in the dead boy's own clothing. The bag, which is being made to figure so conspicuously in the case, bears the name of W. Mason, Derby Road Liverpool. We use it for carrying corn to the horse.

'The hammer, which has been taken possession by the police, is simply a little nail hammer and was seen at the stable several days before the murder. There's nothing suspicious about that. The supposition that the hammer may have been used in driving through the tendons of the lad's joints is, in my opinion, preposterous.

'I think that Barrett's time from Thursday morning till the time the body was found on Saturday can be fully accounted for and that it was impossible for him to have done the deed.

'There's one matter which I think will be a puzzle for the prosecution. It is this: Barrett, on returning from Walmer Villas on the Thursday morning about 8:30, owing to the slipperiness of the streets, had to unyoke his horse in the yard at the dairy and finish the rest of his milk round by hand. The boy Gill did not come with Barrett to the dairy and Barrett himself did not take the horse to the stable, but sent it with a youth about fourteen years of age. Barrett had no occasion of opportunity to go to the stable again on Thursday, until the afternoon.

'It was about half-past eight on the Thursday morning that the boy was missing. Barrett did not bring the lad back with him then, and surely, no one would imagine that the milkman had murdered the lad in plain daylight in the street.

'Then, about the hatchet which the police have taken, it's a common axe for chopping wood. It has never been out of this place at the dairy, and I told them so.

'Before they can implicate Barrett they must be in possession of a good deal more information than the public knows now. They've been making 'a big song' about the evidence to be given by a girl from the Servants' Home, who was closeted with Chief Constable Withers and Chief Detective-Inspector Dobson for an hour on Sunday night at the Town Hall.

'Well, I'm told this girl declares that all she told them at the Town Hall was that she saw a light in the stable one morning about half-past six, and heard some knocking. This would be nothing unusual. The man usually groomed his horse at that hour and could not be expected to do so in absolute silence.

'I may be looked upon as being biased in this matter, but that is not so. The more I reflect over the case, the more I am inclined to believe that Barrett is an innocent man.'

After reading the article himself, Dobson could not help but agree with Withers. It was a very damning article indeed!

That very evening, Withers placed a counter-statement in the evening edition of the local newspapers.

'It must be borne in mind that only three days have elapsed since the news of the murder obtained general circulation. But far from having any cause to feel dispirited, we have every reason to congratulate ourselves on the results of our inquiries. The further we have gone, the more we are convinced that William Barrett is the culprit.

'With regard to the suggestion from some quarters that the criminal must from the state of the body be a butcher or a medical gentleman, this is not supported by the evidence. The first insertion of the knife for the dismemberment of the right leg was made several inches above where the joint was to be found, and the second attempt to find the socket resulted in a gash much too low. It was also obvious that much force had been used.

'Before the next hearing at the police court, we will present evidence that will make this case against William Barrett appear very black indeed.'

THE BRADFORD MURDER AND MUTILATION CASE: SKETCHES AND VIEWS.

WHERE MURDERED BOY LIVED, THORNCLIFFE R?

BARRETT'S STABLE.

BARRETT'S HOUSE - BATEMAN ST.

A MAN SEEN CARRYING SUPPOSED REMAINS.

CHAPTER EIGHT – FRIDAY 4TH JANUARY 1889

Mary Ann and Thomas were finally given the body of their son just after 1:00 p.m. on the following Friday. On their door was now a large laurel wreath festooned with white crepe and ribbons. The blinds to the windows were drawn.

A large crowd had gathered outside 41 Thorncliffe Road, so large that they numbered in the thousands. They were not seeking sensationalism this time. By their sombre demeanour, all dressed in black, it was plain that what had happened to this family had struck a human chord. This was a demonstration of public feeling deeply stirred by the shocking events that had taken place in their neighbourhood. They had come to pay their respects.

The hearse and nine other coaches waited outside the house to start their mournful journey. Pairs of horses stood impatiently pawing at the ground and tossing their heads as their white ostrich feathers moved backwards and forwards in unison. The little white coffin draped with a black cloth lay in a sea of wreaths that could be plainly seen from the large glass windows on all sides. On top of the hearse roof was a carpet of flowers, and a pair of drivers sat perched higher up looking suitably sombre in their black coats and top hats, hands enveloped in white gloves.

There were six pallbearers consisting of the undertaker; two of John's teachers, Mr. Clayton and Mr. Brown; and three of the managers from the school he had attended, Mr. William Jackson, Mr. Samuel Sykes, and Mr. William Farnish. The pallbearers now stood three aside of the hearse, one behind the other, waiting for the family to arrive.

The door opened and suddenly a hushed silence fell over the crowd. Mary Ann emerged wearing a dress of deep black bombazine, her face protected from the outside world by a thick, black veil. It hid her pale face bearing the strain of the last few days; her eyes red raw from lack of sleep and intermittent tears, and it hid too her dishevelled hair. The woman who had always taken pride in her neat appearance and family home no longer cared.

Thomas ushered the three children out of the house along with other family members and put them into the awaiting coaches for the start of the cortege. He took his place behind his son's hearse on foot, alongside other male members of his family and that of Mary Ann's.

A large crowd fell behind the main mourners as the hearse and the nine coaches made their way to the cemetery of Windhill, a small town where Thomas Gill was born and raised.

As the cortege left Thorncliffe Road and turned into Manningham Lane, many of the houses had drawn their blinds over their windows in a show of outward sympathy. Shops were shut all along the route. As the hearse approached, news went on ahead. Men, women, and children lining the streets stood with their heads bowed, hats removed, in silent respect.

The funeral procession continued to grow as they wound their way over the two-mile journey. Mourners from Manningham, Bradford, Windhill, and finally Hipperholme, where Mary Ann's people, the Sharps, came from, were all part of the cortege.

Finally, the hearse and coaches stopped outside Windhill's Wesleyan Chapel. Mary Ann did not see the significant police presence trying to control the surging crowds. Instead, her eyes were fixed on the small coffin with her little Johnny lying inert inside, lying in the dark of which he had always been afraid.

She let out a sob as soon as they removed the coffin from the hearse. Thomas, stone-faced, cradled her with his left arm supporting her as she leaned heavily against him, her head on his chest. They walked like this together following the small white coffin with its silver mountings.

So many people had bought wreaths for Johnny that there were just too many of them for such a small coffin. Instead, they were carefully placed on the floor around the casket during the brief service. One very large and beautiful wreath had been sent from a total stranger; a woman from Bayswater, a Mrs. Evelyn Roberts who had been moved by John's death as far away as London. Other wreaths were from various friends and acquaintances of the Gills, including the cabmen in the employ of Mr. Whittaker, Thomas's boss, and another from the teachers and scholars of the Kirkgate Wesleyan Sunday School.

However, there was one wreath that was the most touching of all, which sat on top of the small coffin alongside the wreath from the family. It was from John's friends of the relatively poor neighbourhood that had been his playground.

Money was hard to come by for these young lads, but they had taken their saved pennies and put them together to buy him a beautiful wreath. On the wreath was a card that read, *'Juvenile Companions.'* The collective wreath was placed just below the neatly finished plate in the centre of the coffin lid.

On it was the simple engraved inscription, *'John Gill, born Feb. 5th, 1881, found dead, Dec. 29th 1888.'*

Several other friends, Alfred Pape from Bateman Street, John Bryce, Frederick Lond, and Joe Watkins, had all forwarded individual wreaths as tributes of respect and affection for the friend they had lost. It was clear to all that were there that young John Gill was indeed someone who had been loved by all who knew him.

Despite the chapel being large and cavernous, the heavy, cloying perfume of the numerous flowers drifted up to mingle with the memories of a boy they had come to bid farewell.

There was not a dry eye in the chapel - and it was full. There were John's relatives and neighbours; friends of his; the three bakers; Mr. Whittaker, Tom's boss; and many of Tom's fellow cabmen. The Kirkgate Wesleyan Sunday School staff and managers, of which John had been a scholar, were also there to pay their respects. So many people had come to pay tribute to the young lad who had touched them in some special way during his brief life.

Throughout the service Mary Ann's tears coursed unchecked, her body wracked with sobs. Thomas's grief had left him feeling numb and hollow. He tried his best to comfort Mary Ann on the one side of him and the rest of his children on the other. They too were having great difficulty coming to terms with the fact that overnight they had gone from four siblings to three.

After the brief service the coffin was carried a short distance to the graveyard on Owlet Road by the staff of the school and the undertaker. Many had walked the two miles from Manningham, and the numbers were such that when the mourners arrived at the graveside, the cemetery was overflowing.

When Mary Ann got to the freshly dug grave, she was inconsolable. When the first clod of soil hit the casket, she was prostrate with grief. Thomas and several other mourners had to restrain her physically from following the coffin, now lying at the depths of the grave. Her ragged emotions and profound grief were painful to those who could only stand and watch, feeling powerless to help in any way.

CHAPTER NINE – TUESDAY 8TH JANUARY 1889

While Withers was preparing for the court case for the coming week the defence team was engaged, yet again, in casting doubt in favour of Barrett.

Hot after the interview given by John Wolfenden, a letter was sent to the editors of the Leeds Mercury and the Yorkshire Post from the church minister of Barrett's parish in Keighley. Both newspapers published the letter on Tuesday.

It was apparent from the letter that Wolfenden, who had been quick to act as judge and juror and swift to boast about funding the court case, had misjudged the cost and length of the case. He was now either not able to, or no longer willing to, be the sole funder for the cause.

The purpose of the published letter was double fold. The first was to encourage others convinced of Barrett's innocence to contribute towards the cost of his defence. The second was to sow further seeds of doubt as to whether he should be convicted or not. Who better to ask than a respected man of the cloth?

'Sir,

'May I, on behalf of very numerous persons in the neighbourhood of Bradford, where the horrible murder of the boy John Gill has lately taken place, ask you to be good enough to insert this letter in your next issue?

'A young man, William Barrett, 23 years of age, has been arrested on the charge of having caused such murder, and he is now in custody, having been remanded by the Bradford magistrates until Wednesday next.

'My object in writing is in nowise to prejudice or anticipate the course of events; but as vicar of the parish where the mother and many of the relatives of the accused reside, I can testify to the high character which they have always borne.

'Everything I have known of William Barrett himself would lead me to discredit the charge now made, unless it were supported by the clearest and most direct evidence. I need hardly point out that up to the present time nothing of such a character has been brought against him before the magistrates.

'He is a working man, and his relations are in the same class. They have voluntarily come forward, and pledged themselves to the cost of the defence to the utmost extent of their means, but there can be no doubt that if the charge be persisted in, those means will not suffice to secure the minute and scientific investigation which the peculiar features of the case demands. Especially considering the unlimited funds the prosecution will have.

'I know that many persons, (especially in the neighbourhood) would be willing to contribute towards that object, and I am therefore prepared to receive and hand over for the purpose of the defence any sums which may be forwarded to me.

'The following gentlemen are also willing to discharge the same duty: Mr. William Spencer, Raygill, Lothersdale, Keighley: the Rev. S Lloyd, 1 Summerset Place, Bradford: Mr. Joshua Fletcher, Cowling, near Keighley, and Mr. A.H. Dawson, Keltus Avenue, Cross Hills, near Keighley.

'Your obedient servant

Withers was in a foul mood. He had been in communication with Mr. Greaves over the last few days trying to get access to the deposition files of which Greaves was the keeper.

Both he and John Craven had applied for these to be released and both parties had been told that they did not have the right to access them.

Despite several meetings with the magistrates and other parties, including a large amount of correspondence between all concerned, the files would not be available to either party. As far as Mr. Greaves was concerned, and he readily quoted Act and Section, that until the investigations were over, and until the case went to the Assizes for trial, the deposition files remained firmly with him.

The second reason for his foul mood was over a letter that had been handed to him by Thomas Gill the previous day. Since the murder, his office had been inundated with crank letters from all over the country. They were either addressed to him personally or to the editors of the local newspapers.

But the letter that he was most angry about was this one. It had been sent to Thomas Gill's home address, with a postmark from Plymouth, signed 'Jack the Ripper'. It was an especially cruel letter, considering what the Gills had gone through. The main contents were making threats to kill his only remaining son, Samuel.

Withers found these letters pernicious. Not long ago he had arrested Maria Coroner for doing the same thing. She was a young Canadian living in Bradford, working as a milliner, and in her spare time writing false letters from 'Jack the Ripper.' Back in October, he had said of Miss Coroner, "To say the least of it, she is a very foolish young woman."

He now wanted to stop this kind of unwelcome correspondence from other quarters and he decided he would do so through public derision and ridicule.

He summoned a reporter from *The Bradford Observer*, who now sat opposite him while he dictated what he wanted to appear in the next edition of the newspaper.

"Over the last few weeks the police at Bradford have received an immense number of letters from correspondents residing in all parts of the country and which, in the character of their contents, sufficiently indicates the morbid mental condition and semi-lunacy of the writers.

"An absurd practice has prevailed of circulating foolish letters under the signature of Jack the Ripper. And among the disreputable writings of this character is a letter that is of a disgraceful nature addressed to the father of the unfortunate boy, John Gill.

"Most of these writers relate remarkable dreams they have had in connection with the murder. Some have pretensions to some prophetic knowledge in connection with the event and some pretend to describe the appearance of the murderer.

"Such a strange crew were never, at one and the same time before, let loose from Bedlam!

"Right, young man, you make sure that you insert that word for word." The reported started to stand up when Withers gestured to him to remain seated.

"It's your lucky day today! I am going to give you some additional information that no one else has at present."

The reporter sat poised on the edge of his chair, eager in anticipation.

"After a lot of investigation we now feel that the stable is not the scene of the murder. We feel that the body was only taken there for the purpose of being mutilated. As such, we have made strenuous efforts to discover where the boy was killed.

"We believe that it could be one of two places and investigations are freshly underway to determine this. We are not at liberty to tell you where these may be, but I can tell you that the area we are looking at is between the limits of Bateman Street, Thorncliffe Road, Ashfield Dairy, the stable of Belle Vue, Walmer Villas, and Bertram Road.

"We would also like to mention that we understand that Mr. Barrett has a certain way with children. We hear that there is a little boy named Stabley, who lives at Kildwick, who is said to have 'cried as if his heart would break' on hearing Barrett had been taken into custody. Therefore, there is no doubt that Mr. Barrett is very fond of children, and they are equally fond of him. We hear too, that he often gives children pennies from time to time, which, no doubt, improves his popularity."

Withers knew exactly what he was doing and he hoped that when people read that, they would begin to see Barrett for the man he was, rather than the man he pretended to be.

He had just finished this last sentence when Dobson walked in.

"James, I wonder if I might have a word with you in private, when you've finished."

"We've just finished, actually. Your timing couldn't have been better."

He shook the reporter's hand and turned his attention to Dobson as the door shut quietly behind them.

Arthur Dobson was already drawing up a chair without being invited to do so; such was the working relationship between these two men.

"I have something here that might brighten up your day considerably."

"Well, that wouldn't be difficult!" Withers retorted sarcastically.

"We've found some witnesses that'll swear that when they walked past the stables at Belle Vue on Thursday night they noticed a lot of water coming from them. So much so, that the drains were overflowing and a lot of water was left on the pavement. If you remember, it was not raining that night so the water that they saw cannot be in dispute."

"That's excellent news!" exclaimed Withers, perking up already.

"And look what we've just found! They were hidden in an ash pit in Thorncliffe Road." With a flourish, Arthur Dobson produced a pair of trousers and a smock from some brown wrapping.

"Don't tell me, Arthur! They've been washed."

"I am afraid so, James. So well washed that some of the fibres have been worn away in the process. They look to fit someone of Barrett's frame but we will have to confirm whether they are his or not."

"Well, Arthur Dobson! I can tell you that my day has just become considerably brighter! Congratulate your men for me and let's see what Rimmington comes up with - when he can. The poor man is rushed off his feet with this case!"

"Rimmington did not have good news regarding his analysis of the debris and the drains from the previous week. Have your heard?" asked Withers.

"No, I haven't."

"Well, not surprising, considering everything else. He said that the tiles were to quote him, 'as clean as a plate' and he found nothing else in the debris. I have to say, Dobson that I am beginning to think that we are working with three crime scenes here.

"The first crime scene is where the boy was killed. I think it had to be a place where Barrett could leave the lad for some time. Perhaps gagged and tied up where he knew it would be secure and he could leave the boy undisturbed for several hours while he carried on doing his milk rounds. We need to look at any empty houses close to Belle Vue.

"The stables at Belle Vue is the second, where the body was dismembered, as he had ready access to water and the butcher's stable is the third, where the body was left.

"Somewhere, within the near vicinity, is the primary crime scene, Arthur. I just hope we find it soon. It has been a very frustrating case but I feel Barrett will have slipped up somewhere. We just have to find that 'somewhere.'"

"Anyway, talking of cases, I guess we'd better get up to the courts to resume the inquest. It's just about time," he said, consulting his pocket watch. "No doubt Craven will be tearing our witnesses to shreds today with relish, as he always does!" he said fairly cheerfully.

By the time they got to the courthouse crowds were already milling. It had become commonplace now for this trial, and the torrential rain that day did not keep them away. Hundreds of men were refused entry due to lack of seats.

James Gaize was the first witness of the day, and soon the courthouse fell silent as the stationmaster at Nottingham Road, Derby took the stand.

"Until last week, I was the ticket collector at the Manningham Station. I remember that on the Thursday the boy went missing I saw the deceased at the station with Barrett at about eight o'clock. He was holding the handle of a can of milk on a barrow that William Barrett was wheeling.

"Just outside the station gate there was a milk cart and a horse, and I last saw the deceased as he and Barrett went towards the cart.

"I saw Barrett again that same evening. He was at the station at about five o'clock. Having heard that the boy Gill was missing, a conversation then took place among the men at the station and at the time, Barrett was there. However, I noticed that Barrett made no comment about the boy during my presence. I found that very perplexing."

Josiah Lee was a milk dealer who took the stand next. After a couple of questions put to him, the jury asked him some questions. In response, he said that when he had called at the dairy at about twenty past nine on the Thursday morning, he saw the cart in the yard, but he did not see Barrett with milk for the dairy as he usually did at that time.

Mr. Coats, the next witness, said that he was a surveyor and had examined the stable at Back Belle Vue. In the course of making a survey of the premises, he had found the part of the ward of a key still in the lock.

Police Constable Kirk took the stand.

"I was working my beat during the nights of the 27th and 28th December when I tried the door of the stables at Back Belle Vue. I found them fast."

"Police Constable Kirk, how is it possible that you found the door fast when the key was missing?" asked Mr. Craven.

"I am not sure. But it was either locked up or propped up, because I tried the door several times and it did not open."

"Exactly when did you try this door?"

"I tried the door every hour, from 10:10 p.m. to 5:10 a.m. the following morning, with the exception of one hour, 12:10 a.m. which was my supper hour. Each time, the door was firmly closed."

"Can you tell the court how you tried opening the door?"

"I tried the handle and then I tried pushing the door open."

Next John Procter Wolfenden took the stand. Withers asked the questions.

"It was Barrett's duty to be at work at the stables at Belle Vue at about half-past six in the morning. He would finish at night at about half-past eight."

"And who was in charge of the keys to the stables, Mr. Wolfenden?"

"The keys to the stable and coach house were generally in Barrett's possession. He was considered to be in charge of the building."

"And is it normal for someone in your employ to work in the stables late at night, say between 10:30 p.m. and 3 a.m.?"

'I am not aware that anyone in my employ had any duties in the stable and coach house that would require them to be there between these hours. There is no gas up there, only the light from candles."

"Mr. Wolfenden. I would like to show you a hammer that was found in your stable, in the roof space of the stable, to be exact. Is it yours?"

"Yes, it is."

"Is it usually kept at the stable?"

"No, it is usually kept at the dairy. I was not aware that it had been taken to the stables."

The witness was then stood down.

Craven had tried to get witnesses to change their statements several times that morning, without success. As things turned out, it was not going particularly well for Craven. Something very important emerged during the cross-examination of Mary Ann Gill that not even Withers could have hoped for.

"Mrs. Gill," began John Craven, "Would I be right in saying that you had allowed your lad to go with the prisoner many times on his rounds?"

"Aye, sir, he went many times."

"Did you at any time feel unsure of, or worried about, your friendship with the prisoner?"

"Not at the time. Johnny liked to go with Willie, an' Willie seemed very fond of the lad."

"So would you say that you trusted the prisoner with your son?"

"Aye, sir, he seemed pleasant enough."

Before Craven could stop her, she went on.

"There wor one occasion though, when Johnny come home one day saying that the prisoner had been fresh with him. An' on another, recently when he told his sisters that during a milk round Willie wor drunk. Willie wor right annoyed with Johnny as the story soon got around the neighbourhood, an' people wor talking about it."

A low buzz, like a swarm of bumblebees, rippled through the courtroom.

"Thank you, Mrs. Gill. That will be all," said Craven abruptly getting rid of Mary Ann as quickly as possible so that she could not do any more damage to his case.

Craven cursed himself for allowing a witness that he was going to cross-examine bring new evidence to light, especially evidence that was contrary to the picture that they had tried so hard to build of Barrett for the public eye.

Withers was beside himself with delight and guessed they had just been given the motive for the murder on a plate. He made no effort in hiding his jubilancy.

Craven sat down and his colleague, Mr. William J. Waugh, took over the questioning. He was hoping that he would have better luck with the next witness, Wilson Riley. Three weeks prior, young Riley had been in the employ of Wolfenden.

"Mr. Riley, did you see the prisoner at all on the day John Gill went missing?"

"Yes, sir. I first saw the accused at about twelve o'clock. His clothes wor wet an' he said that he had been caught in the rain and wor nipping home to change."

"When did you see him again?" asked Waugh.

"He returned to work just after one o'clock."

"Was he wearing clean clothes?"

"Aye, sir. He had changed."

"Did you see the prisoner after that?"

"Because the roads had been slippery, Barrett had left a can of milk at the Manningham Railway Station in the morning. So at one o'clock he took his horse an' cart to fetch it. He wor busy up at the dairy in the afternoon cleaning the milk cans. He then nipped on home for tea an' Elias Smith an' I then had to nip up to the Belle Vue stables to fetch the horse."

"What time was that?"

"About four-thirty."

"Did you notice anything unusual at the stables when you arrived?"

"Nay, sir. Everything looked as it always is."

"And then, what happened then?"

"We left with the horse to fetch the two cans of milk an' returned the morning milk cans. I saw the accused at the station waiting for the train due in at five o'clock. After I got my milk, I left the accused an' went to deliver the evening milk. He wor with two young boys who helped him, Elias Smith an' Jesse Paget."

"Was that the last time you saw the accused?"

"No, sir. After my round I come back to the dairy at about 7:30 p.m. where Mr. Barrett wor still doing his duties. He wor separating the cream from the milk in the cellar. After that, the accused then took his horse an' returned it to the stables. He then come back to the dairy after about twenty-five minutes an' asked me to nip on home an' sit with him as his wife wor going out. We nipped down to his house at about 8:30 p.m. After that, I went home with him an' wor there until about 9:30 p.m. when his wife returned."

"And you saw the prisoner on the Friday, after that?"

"Aye, sir. I saw him at about 7:00 a.m. an' he wor doing his daily duties. I wor also up at the stables an' saw nothing out of the ordinary."

"Did you notice anything out of the ordinary with regards to the prisoner's behaviour on either Thursday or Friday?"

"Nay. Nothing at all, sir."

"How long has the stable key been missing?" enquired Waugh.

"Several days before the Thursday, sir."

"Has the key since been found?"

"Nay, sir."

"So, would you say that it was possible that anyone could have access to the stable then during this time Mr. Riley?"

"Aye, sir. It's possible."

"Your witness, Mr. Freeman," said Waugh, turning to James Freeman, who declined to cross-examine at this stage.

Waugh was just warming up. He decided that it was time to hound some of the other witnesses. He went through several of those who said that they had seen Barrett with the boy long after he had left him. All of them were consistent in their statements. Just as he was losing hope, he called Annie Beal to the stand.

"Miss. Beal, please relay to the court what you think you saw on the morning of Thursday, 27th December when your milk was being delivered," asked Waugh, his voice laced with a touch of scorn.

"It wor just after 8:30 a.m. when I saw the prisoner with a lad inside."

"Are you sure about the time?"

"Aye, sir, quite sure, I remember it quite distinctly."

"You were not certain about the prisoner that it was him?"

"Aye, I am."

"Were you certain the first time before the magistrates?"

"Aye, so far as I can remember."

Waugh saw his opportunity. "Then you had some difficulty in remembering?"

"Aye."

"What has refreshed your memory since?"

"I don't know if there's anything particular," replied Annie, feeling the pressure.

"Will you please tell me what has refreshed your memory since?" Waugh was now badgering, and Annie Beal felt at a loss of what to say.

He continued his attack on her.

"No? What is it?"

"It's nothing." She finally replied.

"Then your memory is no better today than when you were before the magistrates?" he asked belligerently.

Annie's mouth was drying up and her hands were clammy. She felt panicked but said nothing.

"Is that so?" asked Waugh a little louder.

"It is so," she said feeling confused, no longer remembering the original question.

"And you were then in doubt as to whether the prisoner was the man who was with the cart?"

Annie quickly recovered.

"That wor the man with the cart." She pointed to Barrett.

"Had you some doubt as to whether the prisoner was the man or not?"

Annie did not want to give a wrong answer, yet again.

Waugh took her silence for indecisiveness.

"Didn't you say you had some difficulty, when first before the magistrates in recognising this man?"

"That wor the man I saw in the cart." Annie's answer was firm.

"That is not my question," rebuked Waugh. "Didn't you say you had some difficulty, when first before the magistrates, in recognising this man? Yes or no? Is it true that you had some difficulty?"

"Nay."

"Is it not true that you ever said so? Didn't you say before the magistrates, 'So far as I can remember the prisoner was the man?'"

Annie, a simple soul, feeling the pressure of being on the stand, and not always understanding the questions put to her, fell headlong into the trap.

"Aye, that is it."

Waugh slapped his thigh in delight.

"And now tell me, Miss. Beal, who was driving the cart?"

"That, I cannot say for sure. But I'm sure that the lad wor in the cart, as I wor standing there for about five or six minutes."

"Can you tell me how you identified the lad?"

"By his hair and clothing."

"What was there peculiar about the boy's clothing you noticed that morning?"

"He had a little blue top coat. There wor nothing peculiar that I know of, only he wor pretty well wrapped up."

At this stage, the Chairman of the court interrupted. "Did you notice his features?"

"I did not especially."

"Did you notice sufficient to identify the boy afterwards?" he asked.

"Aye, sir."

Waugh was losing interest in this witness and Annie Beal was relieved when she was told that she could stand down.

Barrett remained standing and he had listened closely to all that had transpired. His demeanour was now very different. Yesterday, Detective King had formally charged him with the murder of John Gill. He had not slept well. His eyes were dull, and he was looking strained and tired.

While the inquest was going on more reporters were tramping all over Cross Hills trying to find out more about Willie Barrett and the person he was. A local reporter wrote the following:

'An inquiry was made among the inhabitants of Cross Hills, Glasburn, and Cononley this week as to what sort of man William Barrett was. On every hand, we heard nothing but what was favourable to his character. Everybody who knows him speaks of him as a kind-hearted and most sweet-tempered young man.

'The story which has been set afloat with regard to insanity having existed in this Barrett family is a matter which is entirely unknown to anyone in the district, and it appears to have not the slightest foundation, in fact, whatsoever. No one in the Barrett family or the Boocock family – for this is really the name of Barrett's ancestors – has been known to be weak-minded.

'The story may have arisen out of the following circumstances. The name Barrett sometimes spelled as Barrit, is a common one in the neighbourhood of Cross Hills and the existence of insanity is in another family of the same name of Barrett, two members of which have recently died in the Skipton Workhouse. This may explain this groundless story about the prisoner's ancestors.

'The statement that the prisoner was subject to violent fits of passion, and had been known to strike animals without the slightest provocation, appears to be unworthy of the slightest credence.

'Persons who have known him from an early childhood say that they have never seen him in a passion and that a better-tempered youth it was hardly possible to meet with, in fact, as one person very characteristically put it, "He could not hurt a mouse."

'He seems to have been passionately fond of children. Mrs. Shuttleworth of Cononley, for whose husband the prisoner worked for some time, states that her two children were never happy without they were in his company, and on many occasions, he has given them copper pennies.

'Another instance is that of a boy named Stabley, living near the Kildwick Station. He states that when Barrett was working on Mr. Wolfenden's farm he went about with him repeatedly. All the time he never heard him swear, nor use an angry word.

'Unfortunately, Barrett's father is dead. His mother, sisters, and brothers are all spoken of being highly respectable and of a very industrious turn of mind.

'Barrett, too, is regarded as a very intelligent and hardworking man and this seems to be proved by the fact that after he had left Mr. Wolfenden's service that gentleman was willing to take him back.

'In his youth, he attended the Primitive Methodist Sunday School at Cononley, in which he was a Sunday school teacher for several years until he removed from the village.

'He became connected in marriage with a most respectable and well-known family, having married a sister of Mr. George Unwin Metcalfe, printer, of Cross Hills.'

CHAPTER TEN – WEDNESDAY 9TH
JANUARY 1889

At 9:30 a.m. the coroner, Mr. James Gwynne Hutchinson, and the jury assembled at Town Hall to discuss the inquest. In the room, in addition, to the coroner and the jury, were Mr. Freeman, Mr. Craven, and Superintendent Campbell who was representing the police.

Superintendent Campbell opened up the discussion.

"Gentlemen, I have to tell you that we are not prepared to go on with the case as it stands. The case is far from being completed before the magistrates and it would, therefore, be necessary to have a further adjournment for the Coroner's Inquest."

"Superintendent, while I understand your position, I have to say that this will no doubt be exceedingly inconvenient to the jury," replied Mr. Hutchinson.

Some of the jurors were nodding in agreement, and others were saying, "Hear! Hear!" under their breath.

He continued, "However, as the case is coming up before the magistrates this morning, an application for an adjournment is a reasonable one, and I believe ought to be acceded to. It is my intention when the inquest is resumed to go on with the case until it reaches a conclusion," said Mr. Hutchinson.

John Whipp Craven interjected. "I would like to point out that we have managed to gather a considerable amount of evidence which the police has obtained, but has not been called for. I feel that it is only right that the jury should have this information."

"If that is the case, I am willing to postpone the inquest until next Friday. Does that suit everyone?"

Some of the jurors were not very happy, but in the end, it was agreed that the Coroner's Inquest would duly be postponed.

Later in the morning, William Barrett came up again in court to appear at the Magistrate's Inquest.

Felix Rimmington, the Bradford borough analyst, was first up on the stand.

"Mr. Rimmington, have you concluded your examination, including the items sent to you by Chief Constable Withers and his staff?"

"I have."

"Can you tell the court your findings?"

"I analysed the contents from the boy's stomach and found farinaceous food, and a few currants. This led me to the conclusion that what he had eaten was currant cake."

"Would that be the same currant cake that was found in the kitchen of Mrs. Barrett?"

"It was definitely currant cake, but whether it was the exact currant cake found in the Barrett kitchen is difficult to say."

"Mr. Rimmington, what do you conclude from your examination of the three rags that were found?"

"The cloths that were found in the stables were examined very carefully. However, the results were inconclusive.

"I have a strong suspicion that blood had at some stage been on the rags, but unfortunately, I was not able to prove this distinctly. Under a microscope, I did discover small particles resembling coagulant matter, which indicates the possible presence of blood. However, upon further examination of these particulars I could not satisfy myself that they were blood. This was mainly because the rag appeared to have been soaked in water and well rinsed. This therefore diminished the chances of obtaining any definite evidence."

"And the canvas wrapper?"

"Yes, the wrapper was also examined for blood but again I found no evidence. The piece of print was wet when I examined it and it appeared to have been much wetter previously when I first received it. I found no trace of blood on that either. On the piece of canvas, there was only one spot that was red and suspicious, but I was not able to prove the actual presence of blood.

"The knife, hammer, and hatchet were also examined - all with negative results. On the knife there was a mark which turned out to be rust and in the crevice a piece of matter which I found to be ordinary fat."

"You also examined the clothes the prisoner had in his house, which were retrieved after the search?"

"Yes, there was a sleeved-waistcoat and a pair of trousers belonging to the prisoner. I found no blood on the waistcoat that had been recently washed. Again, this is a circumstance that would increase the difficulty concerning the indication of the presence of blood. If soda and soap had been used in the washing of any spots there, any bloodstains would have been obliterated.

"The corduroy trousers were quite clean and dry but when I saw them on Monday last they seemed as if they too had been recently washed. I did cut pieces off the trousers where I saw marks but again, I did not found any blood on them."

"Your witness," said Mr. Freeman.

Mr. Waugh did not cross-examine Mr. Rimmington. Instead, he said, "I am very much obliged to you, Mr. Rimmington."

Next on the stand was Doctor Samuel Lodge.

"I visited Back Mellor Street on the morning of the 29th December and saw the disjointed remains of the boy Gill lying on the ground in the stable yard.

"In the afternoon of the same day I made a post-mortem examination of the body with Doctor Major and Mr. Miall present. In my opinion, a deep stab wound to the chest caused death. Because of the examination, I found certain parts of the body previously thought missing, including portions of certain bones and a portion of the private parts, but not all.

"It is my belief that the boy was not murdered on the spot where the body was discovered. Death must have been instantaneous and the mutilation must have taken place immediately afterwards. The body was quite bloodless and had the appearance of having been well washed and drained.

"The mutilations could not have been accomplished by one instrument alone. The principle instrument must have been a sharp, strong, pointed, and well-tempered knife. A bread knife may have been employed to inflict the two chest wounds but in order to sever some of the limbs, considerable force must have been used, for instance, the force from a hammer or mallet.

"The shirt of the deceased had the appearance of being stained with blood and water although I am not absolutely sure on this. There was definitely a stain but it was not just of blood."

"Thank you, Doctor Lodge. Mr Waugh?"

"Doctor Lodge, is there a limit of time, in which, or before which, death must have taken place, judging from the condition of the body?" asked Waugh.

"I should not like to say," said Lodge. "I have some uncertainty."

"You could not say how many hours the boy had been dead?"

"I cannot say with certainty, but to the best of my knowledge, I would put it at about forty hours. However, it may have been shorter, or even longer than that. I won't say it was within twelve hours. My impression is that it was within twenty-four hours from the time I first saw the body, but I won't be bound by that, as I would be sorry if I misled the Bench."

"Are you of the opinion, Doctor Lodge, that the person who removed the ears of the boy must have been a person of considerable skill?"

"The operation was done as cleanly as I could have done it myself. The same remark would apply to the way in which the private parts had been removed."

"You found the body ripped up?"

"Yes, it was cut through to the breastbone."

"Thank you, Doctor Lodge. Your Worships, I would like to call Doctor Herbert Major to the stand."

"Doctor Major, you were present during Doctor Lodge's post-mortem of the boy, Gill?"

"That is correct."

"What, in your opinion, was the cause of death?"

"Cause of death was due to the wounds to the chest area. The upper wound, if inflicted first, would have caused instant death. The lower wound, if inflicted first, would have caused rapid but not instant death."

Mr. Freeman excused the witness and then turned to the magistrates, "That is my case, Your Worships, and on the evidence before you I submit that you have no alternative but to commit the prisoner for trial."

Mr Armitage, the spokesman for the magistrates, addressed the court.

"Gentlemen, we will retire now and review the case, after which we will adjourn for lunch. We will reassemble at three o'clock."

At three o' clock, the court filled up quicker than it had emptied some hours before. There was a lot of excitement in the courthouse and low murmurs were heard among the men as opinions were passed back and forth.

"All rise!"

Once everyone was re-seated, Mr. Armitage cleared his throat before he began. The room fell silent.

"The Bench feels, to the fullest extent, the great importance of their duty upon this occasion. They have carefully considered every point of the evidence and they are unanimously of the opinion that no *prima facie* case has been made out."

Barrett was clutching the rail in front of him so hard that his knuckles were white. He was not sure what *prima facie* was. However, he certainly understood the next sentence.

"The prisoner will be discharged."

For those believing in Barrett's guilt, it was a bitter blow. This was particularly so for Chief Constable Withers, Chief Detective-Inspector Dobson, and some of their men who were present. James Withers was devastated. However, Barrett had many supporters present who believed he was innocent. A thunderous applause erupted. The noise was deafening within the confined space.

Armitage soon had to strike the gavel.

"Order! Order!" he commanded. However, it was a lost cause. Even the police officials present could not quell the crowd. After a while, the noise subsided and Mr. Waugh got to his feet.

"I would like to thank the magistrates for their care and attention that they have awarded to this case, and for the unfailing courtesy they have shown both to myself and to Mr. Craven, my friend and colleague. It has, without a doubt, been a most difficult task and I would like to extend my thanks to Mr. Freeman. He has shown courtesy and fairness in a case that has been very difficult. So, thank you gentlemen, all of you." With that, he sat down.

The Chairman addressed the court next. "Thank you, Mr. Waugh. The Magistrates were just doing their duty, but we thank you for the recognition."

The courtroom emptied and large numbers of people assembled outside the Town Hall waiting for William Barrett to exit. News had soon spread that Barrett was a free man and spectators came in their droves. As soon as people heard that Barrett was about to appear the cheers went up, but it turned out to be a false start. There were several false alarms until someone in the crowd suddenly shouted, "Yon's him!"

The crowd surged forward towards the cab stand in Market Street, which turned out to be a decoy, for while the crowds were thus engaged, Barrett, Wolfenden, and Barrett's brother emerged from Town Hall and climbed into a waiting cab fairly undetected and escaped the crowds rather skilfully. However, some managed to catch up to the departing vehicle and ran behind it for a while. They cheered as he hung a red handkerchief out of the cab window in acknowledgement, until the cab picked up speed, leaving them all behind. They stood and watched as it turned into Manningham Lane going towards the premises of his now former employer, John Procter Wolfenden.

When Barrett arrived at Ashfield Dairy, a large gathering that had quickly formed eagerly applauded him. He shook hands with the well-wishers and then disappeared into the narrow building.

Wolfenden had offered him his old job back in Bradford. He had also said that if he did not care to remain in the area after what had transpired, he totally understood. The other option was that he would find work for Barrett in Kildwick, as an alternative. Barrett had given the matter much thought during his detention and had already decided on what he would do. He was about to tell Wolfenden that he had settled on the second option.

CHAPTER ELEVEN – FRIDAY 18TH JANUARY 1889

Although Barrett was a free man, and the Magistrate's Inquest was over, dismissing the case had no bearing on the Coroner's Inquest, initiated by Mr. John Gwynne Hutchinson some weeks ago. Court resumed on the Friday afternoon.

William Barrett was not present, but his lawyer, Mr. John Craven, was still representing him, albeit with some reluctance.

Many of the witnesses who had been called were recalled. Some gave the same information, while at other times new information became known. However, nothing emerged that was of any great significance, that was, until Joseph Bucke took the stand again.

When asked by the coroner if he had noticed any marks on the floor that would have, or could have, been made by a barrow in transporting the body, Bucke said that he had not noticed such a mark. Back Mellor Street was not paved in places, he said, and if the remains of the deceased had been brought up in a barrow, he would have noticed such a mark on the ground. He had not.

Mary Ann, still distraught nearly three weeks after losing her eldest child, gave further evidence.

"Mrs. Gill, did William Barrett help to look for your boy when you thought that he was lost?" asked Mr. Hutchinson.

"Nay, sir, I wor not aware that Barrett had looked for the lad, nor did he offer to either myself or my husband his assistance to search for him."

"Mrs. Gill, was the deceased insured?"

"Aye, sir, we paid one pence per week."

"For what amount?"

"Five pounds."

"Is that all the money he was insured for?"

"Aye, sir."

"And was there any sum of £100 or anything else at interest for him?"

At this stage, the coroner interjected to simplify the question, "Any money payable on his death?"

"Nay, sir."

The coroner persisted with his line of questioning, "Nobody derives any pecuniary benefit from the death?"

"None, that I'm aware of," replied Mary Ann.

Thomas Gill then took the stand. He was a shadow of his former self. The spark had gone out of his eyes. He had also lost a lot of weight over the last few weeks. He was now being questioned by Chief Constable Withers.

"Mr. Gill, was your lad insured?"

"Aye, sir, for five pounds. We took that money an' paid it towards his funeral."

"Was there anyone who would derive any pecuniary benefit from the death?"

"Other than the five pounds, nay, sir."

"Thank you, Mr. Gill. You may now stand down. I next call Mr. Boyes."

"Mr. Boyes, please state your full name, address and profession."

"My name is William Boyes, and I live in Salt Street. I am a barber."

"Did you see William Barrett and the deceased on the Thursday he went missing?"

"I did. I wor doing some business in Laburnum Street on the Thursday after Christmas Day, at about nine o'clock in the morning, when I saw William Barrett an' his cart. In his company wor a little lad, but I did not notice who he wor. Barrett's cart wor standing at the end of the street."

John Craven had been sitting impatiently drumming his fingers on the desk. He could not believe that he was listening to all this nonsense yet again while the magistrates had exonerated his client.

He rose and addressed those present, his voice tinged with exasperation.

"Gentlemen, I have sat here patiently listening to these witnesses and really don't see the point of even cross-examining them, considering that my client has already been discharged from custody.

"I will certainly place myself in the hands of the court if there is any *new* information that is brought before them, or if any witness may throw some light upon the case, and this I welcome.

"But until such time, gentlemen, I would like to say, on behalf of Mr. Barrett, that he has had a perfect case. I hope you will allow me to say, with the greatest respect to the court, due to all that has gone before, that Mr. Barrett does not appear again on this charge."

Mr. Hutchinson was quick to respond.

"Mr. Craven, I do not wish you to think that I do not want you to appear and represent your client's interests. It is, let me remind you, your duty to probe such a matter as this, to the very bottom. However, at the same time I cannot allow questions that have no bearing on the case, to be asked.

"As far as I am concerned, I am very pleased that you have availed yourself to the inquest and I hope that you will continue to assist in the inquiring by remaining."

Craven was not so easily swayed.

"Sir, I am obliged to you, however, I do feel that unless I can cross-examine the witnesses with some hope of success with regards to the defence, if it should be necessary, it really is entirely useless."

The coroner was becoming increasingly irritated.

"Mr. Craven, if you desire to render services to the inquiry then you had better remain in the court and represent your client."

John Craven sat down promptly, glowered, but said no more.

After several of the old witnesses had taken the stand, many only rehashing what had already been told, the court adjourned at 6:30 p.m. to reconvene the following week.

On the 15th Jan 1889, there was another Jack the Ripper letter sent to the C Division of the Metropolitan Police in which the writer claimed:

'I ripped up a little boy in Bradford...'

Another letter was sent the following day:

'I am still in London after my trip to Bradford.'

CHAPTER TWELVE – TUESDAY 22ND JANUARY 1889

On the 14th January, just days after William Barrett's case was dismissed by the magistrates' court an application was made by the Keighley law firm, Messrs. W. & G Burr & Co. The letter was written on behalf of William Barrett asking the Bradford Town Council for compensation in favour of Barrett for the expenses he had incurred due to the wrongful charges brought against him.

The reply came in the form of a public letter published in several of the local newspapers and written by the Town Clerk of Bradford, Mr. William Thomas McGowan.

'Dear Sirs,

I am directed by the Chairman of the Watch Committee to acknowledge receipt of your letter, of the 14th inst., and in reference thereto I am to state that, however painful the circumstances surrounding the case may be, it appears to the committee the police have throughout acted in the best of their judgement in the honest discharge of their duty, and that neither they, nor the local authority are answerable for the result of the proceedings before the Borough Bench; more especially as the officers of the Treasury thought it right and proper to take up the prosecution.

'I have to add that the committee fully appreciate the courteous tone of your communication, although they cannot concur in the view you present of the business.

'I am, dear Sirs, yours truly, W.T. McGowen.

CHAPTER THIRTEEN – FRIDAY 25ᵀᴴ JANUARY 1889

The John Gill case was certainly turning into a very frustrating one for those wanting to bring the perpetrator to justice. It certainly had not been a case without high drama.

On Friday afternoon, after the Coroner's Inquest had resumed, Mr. John Craven was nowhere in sight. On inquiring where he was, the court was told that he was unavoidably detained on business in London. His father, Mr. Joseph Craven, would be representing Barrett in his stead.

James Hutchinson sincerely doubted that that was the case, in light of what had happened the previous week, but there was little he could do about it other than grudgingly accept Craven's apologies, and move on with the case without him.

His mood did not improve when halfway through the proceedings a letter was handed to the Foreman of the Jury, Mr. Gaskarth, who passed the letter on to Mr. Hutchinson.

"It is from Doctor Hime, sir," explained Gaskarth as he passed the letter further up the line.

"Doctor Hime?"

Gaskarth nodded. "It is related to the inquiry, Your Worship."

Hutchinson opened the letter that had been previously sealed and read the contents.

'January 25, 1889.

54 Horton Road.

'Dear Sir,

I beg to repeat on my own behalf what was stated by Mr. Craven at the Coroner's Court last week, viz.: That if there is any information derived from the post-mortem examination of the unfortunate little boy Gill, or from other sources which you may think of use, I shall be happy to place it at your disposal.

'I feel that the failure to bring the criminal to justice is no less a misfortune than the cruel murder he has perpetuated. Some of the evidence of Doctor Roberts and myself is in direct conflict with the medical evidence already laid before you in this case and consequently opposes the conclusion founded on this portion of evidence.

'I am, dear Sir, yours truly,

'Thomas Whiteside Hime.'

"This is preposterous and highly irregular!" spat Hutchinson as he finally finished reading the letter. His eyes sought out Thomas Hime in the gallery and directed his next scathing comment directly at him, once he had found him.

"And it is with regret, Doctor Hime, that you do not know any better by forwarding this letter through the channels of the foreman. I am going to discredit this correspondence and any other correspondence that comes to me via such channels."

"Mr. Withers, do you have a new witness?" he snapped.

"I do, Your Worship. A statement was made by a witness about nine or ten days ago."

"Is this the Salvation Army man?" he asked, impatiently.

Withers felt that he had better divulge his misgivings about this new witness so that there were no repercussions later on.

"Your Worship, the witness does belong to the Salvation Army, however, to be honest, he makes use of certain expressions that at times would lead one to the conclusion that there was something questionable about his intellect. However, because this person made a statement, I felt it my responsibility to say that perhaps there could be something valuable in what he had stated.

"In order for his statement to be relied on, I had the witness seen by three individual medical men for an assessment. Each of them tell me that he is capable of understanding the situation and giving evidence."

"I do not want their opinion, Mr. Withers," was Hutchinson's derisive reply. "I want the witness in the box and then I can judge for myself!"

John Thomas Dyer ambled into the courthouse. He said that he was of Longland Street and was a labourer, occasionally working for Major Churchill.

"Please tell the court, Mr. Dyer what you said you saw."

"On the Saturday following Christmas Day I wor going to Major Churchill's house an' left home at about five minutes to six. I went straight up Lumb Lane an' turned down the back of Belle Vue. Whilst passing the house formerly occupied by Doctor Denby I saw the milkman Barrett, whom I know quite well, coming out of a little door next to the Orphan's Home, which opened into Back Belle Vue. He had a parcel that he carried in front of him. At the time, I was quite near to him."

Hutchinson interrupted. "Did you know him?"

"Aye, I knew him by his walk. He used to tease me on Manningham Lane about the Salvation Army. I went over to the other side so that I could look into his face because I always used to talk to him. He delivered milk next door to Major Churchill's."

"Did you speak to him?" asked Hutchinson.

"Aye, I said, 'Good morning, Sir. Bless the Lord! Hallelujah!' but he didn't say anything. He hung down his head. He walked straight down Belle Vue, an' I followed him into Manningham Lane. On reaching Manningham Lane, Barrett crossed the road an' nipped down a snicket opposite the end of Belle Vue next to the bicycle shop. I didn't see what became of him, it being rather misty, an' I went on the left-hand side of the lane to Major Churchill's."

"Have you any doubt about the man being Barrett?"

"Nay. I know him by being in the yellow milk cart."

"And you are sure of that?"

"Aye."

"Do you wish to ask any questions of the witness, Mr. Withers?"

"No, that is the plain statement."

"Mr. Craven?"

Old man Craven got to his feet with some difficulty, but where his body was failing him his mind was still as sharp as a razor.

"How old are you, Mr. Dyer?"

"I'm twenty years old, sir," he said optimistically. "Although I do not know what year I wor born in."

"Do you know how to get to know?" Joseph Craven asked sarcastically.

"By nipping down to the Register Office."

A ripple of laughter went around the court.

"Do you know this year?"

"Nay, sir."

"You have been in a court before?"

"Yes, four years ago, an' also last year as a witness."

"Do you remember having been here any other time?"

"Aye, sir, eight years ago."

"What were you there for then?"

"I wor locked up for being with bad boys."

"How long did they keep you?"

"Two years and six months," came the quick reply.

"Where were you sent?"

"To the reformatory school."

"And were you not much taught there?" he asked incredulously.

"Not so much, because I wor out on the farm."

"Did they teach you figures?"

"I wor put into the second standard, an' then put back again because they couldn't teach me nothing," he said with candour.

There was more laughter in the courtroom.

"How many days after Christmas was it that you say you saw the man?"

"On the Saturday after."

"What time did you leave home that morning?"

"About five minutes to six. An' I got into Belle Vue about six-twenty. An' then I nipped on to Major Churchill's about six-thirty."

"Did you go on Wednesday?"

"Nay, I didn't. An' I didn't go on Thursday."

"Did you go on Friday?"

"Nay, I ought to have, but I missed and went on Saturday instead."

"How do you remember it was Saturday?"

"Because I know," was the stubborn reply. "I'm sure it wor because it was the same day I got thrupence as a Christmas box."

"Does anybody else tease you?"

"Lots of people," Dyer admitted.

"Why?"

"Because they think I'm a bit silly."

The coroner interjected.

"You do not know their thoughts. You judge them."

Dyer, who had spent his whole life being teased, taunted and tormented by others felt justified in his reply.

"Well, I judge so," he replied swiftly and firmly.

Mr Craven senior asked Dyer, "Are you sure it was Barrett?"

"Aye, an' I crossed over to the other side of the road to look an' be sure. On that morning, he had on a pair of cord trousers."

"How do you know?"

"Because I wor looking on the ground."

"What sort of a hat had he on?"

"I didn't notice. I didn't notice anything else Barrett had on except his trousers, which wor a little dirty. When Barrett came out of the stable door, he held the bundle under one arm an' shut the door with the other. The bundle appeared to be a very heavy one. I didn't take notice of the colour of the bundle, but it wor wrapped up like a bundle of clothes. I didn't notice what it wor wrapped in. He didn't run, but he went faster than me, an' as he went along he wor leaning down with the bundle in front of him."

"Did you see him cross Manningham Lane?"

"Aye, I did, sir."

"Where were you when you saw him get to the other side of Manningham Lane?"

"I wor at the bottom of Back Belle Vue."

"When he was on the other side, where was Mrs. Cooper?"

Dyer hesitated just for a fraction and continued. "Nay, I didn't see Mrs. Cooper. I know nothing about Mrs. Cooper."

"Who did you first tell about this?"

"I told the cook at Major Churchill's about three days after.

"And when did you tell the police?"

"I never told the police. I don't know who told them."

"When did you first see the police?"

"I told them about three weeks since; a day or two before Barrett got off."

"Mr. Dyer, how far were you able to see Barrett going down the snicket?"

"Not very far. I could see him nipping down to the snicket because there wor a lighted lamp there but I worn't able to see him after that."

"Why did you not come to the police and make a report with what you had seen immediately after the event?"

"Well, because I'd told several people but nobody took any notice of what I'd told them."

"Did you know the deceased?"

"I only knew the deceased from seeing him in Barrett's milk cart but I never knew he wor missing until after I'd heard about the murder."

"Mr. Dyer," asked Craven, "were you promised any remuneration, any money, for giving evidence here today?"

"Nay, sir, I wor not, nor do I want any." After this last comment, laughter was now heard within the ranks of the jury.

"Finally, Mr. Dyer, other than Barrett wearing dirty cord trousers, can you remember what else he was wearing?"

"He had a coat on, sir."

"Thank you, Mr. Dyer. That will be all."

As it was announced that the inquest would be adjourned until February 4th the foreman of the jury, Mr. Gaskarth rose to speak.

"Your Worship, on behalf of the jury, we have all expressed a desire to hear from Mr. Barrett himself, and call him as a witness. So far, during this case he has not been called to the stand and we feel that this needs to be remedied."

Mr. Hutchinson responded. "Mr. Gaskarth, while I understand your interest in hearing Mr. Barrett's side of the story the matter rests with his legal advisors. At this stage they have decided not to put Mr. Barrett on the stand."

Mr. Craven stood up shuffled some pages and hurriedly left the building without making any comment or elucidating any further.

CHAPTER FOURTEEN – MONDAY 28TH JANUARY 1889

John Thomas Dyer was a crucial key witness. It was his testimony alone that linked all the other circumstantial evidence together, to make it one cohesive whole. Withers knew all too well that yesterday the defence had tried to discredit his intellect, along with the credibility of his testimony. As a result, he had asked Dyer to be examined by Doctor Major and the following appeared in the newspapers around the country.

'In reference to the mental capacity of the witness Dyer, Doctor Major, who was formerly the medical superintendent of the Lunatic Asylum at Wakefield, has certified to the following effect:

"Having this day made an examination of the mental state of John Thomas Dyer, I am of the opinion that while he is probably of a somewhat low type of general intelligence. Yet he is not an imbecile; that he is clear and rational on matters within his knowledge; that he is free from morbid excitement or other symptoms of insanity, and that he understands the nature and responsibility of evidence in a court of justice. I am therefore of the opinion that the said John Thomas Dyer is competent to give such evidence regarding the circumstances of which he may have cognisance."

'Mr. Samuel Lodge and Doctor Philip Miall have also certified to the following effect:

"He is evidently a person whose intellect is below the average quality. There is not before us any symptom of brain diseases, such as epilepsy or other periodical affection. There is

every appearance of truthfulness about the man. There is no apparent desire to enlarge or speak on any subject under discussion extravagantly. Simplicity appears to be his prevailing characteristic, and he seems to be able to make a simple statement on any facts within his limited knowledge."

'We hope that this will dispel the rumours that Dyer is an incompetent witness.'

John Thomas Dyer had now been elevated to an important material witness.

CHAPTER FIFTEEN – MONDAY 4TH FEBRUARY 1889

The Coroner's Inquest resumed on Monday. It had been a long, protracted case and many of the jurors were relieved that they could finally see the end in sight.

Harry Ledgard was a new witness. He was a photographer who stated that on the Thursday after Christmas he was returning home by way of Back Belle Vue at about 10:30 p.m. when passing the stable he noticed that the door was open. There was a light inside, and he saw a man opposite the door standing in a stooped position.

Emma Turrell, who was a cook in the service of Major Churchill at 12 Walmer Villas, was called on to speak about what Dyer had told her. Under cross-examination, she said that Dyer had made a communication to her on the Wednesday before Barrett was released.

"What was the communication Dyer made to you, Miss. Turrell?" asked John Craven.

"It wor relative to the deceased boy, Gill. He told me he wor nipping down Back Belle Vue when he saw Barrett coming out of the stable carrying a bundle. He saw Barrett cross the tramlines an' went down by the bicycle shop. He said he greeted Barrett but he didn't return the greeting."

"What part of the day was it when Dyer told you this?"

"It wor late in the evening, about ten o'clock."

"Did he say anything to you about the trial that day?"

"Nay, he did not."

"And that is all he said about it?"

"Aye, that's all."

"You feel quite certain that it was Wednesday?"

"Aye, I am certain."

The coroner decided to ask her a question. "Where did he tell you this?"

"At Major Churchill's in the kitchen."

"Was there anyone else present?"

"The housemaid an' a friend named Jane Ferguson."

Constable Withers said, "We understand that he was meant to work earlier on in the week, but failed to do so. Is that correct?"

"Aye, I'd asked him on the Friday to come early on Saturday morning. Dyer left Mr. Churchill's at about half-past eight in the evening an' had not yet heard about the murder. I myself did not hear of the discovery until after ten o'clock, later that night."

Next up was Gertrude Mary Williams, of Birkenshaw, the aunt of Nellie Pearson, who had given testimony earlier on in the case. She remembered that the Thursday after Christmas her niece, after spending time with her, left at five minutes to nine to catch the nine-fifteen train for Bradford.

With no more witnesses to be called, or cross-examined, Mr. Hutchinson, borough coroner and qualified solicitor, finally addressed the court on the facts brought before them.

"Members of the jury, there will be no difficulty in determining the cause of death in this case, as the medical testimony has clearly defined. The important question you have to consider is whether the evidence that you have now heard is sufficient to fix responsibility on any one person.

"In cases of this character, where there is no direct evidence to show by whose hand the terrible deed was done, it then becomes necessary to fall back on what is known as circumstantial evidence. This is done by putting together a chain of circumstances that when reasonably considered, fix culpability and guilt upon any person.

"In cases where that character has to be relied on, it is usual in the first place to trace the deceased person to the period and place when last seen alive, or known to be alive, or in other words, to fix the company of the deceased person.

"In this case, the evidence points to the fact, indeed it was not denied, that the boy was last seen alive in the company of William Barrett. Whether it was ten minutes to ten or half-past eight according to the admissions made on two, if not three occasions by Barrett himself, the deceased was last seen alive in his company.

"We have heard the movements of Mr. Barrett over the last few weeks, as well as the movements of the boy from the moment he left home to the time he was last seen. Coming to the evidence of Miss Pearson, this is, in my opinion, evidence of the greatest importance, because of the times that she gave and the fact that she knew the boy well that had delivered milk to her on several occasions.

"If her statements were true, and she brought her aunt from Birkenshaw to corroborate her statement, then the statements made by Barrett were deliberate untruths.

"The jury would please to remember that when I came to refer to the time for which Barrett came to recount the time, ten minutes to ten o'clock was an important element because Barrett said that he left the deceased a long time before that.

"That Barrett afterwards went to the dairy and after that to the stable to put his horse up, there can be no doubt. Was the child ever seen again afterwards? No, he was not. He was lost sight of and never seen again until his mutilated remains were found.

"When we look at the statements given by Miss. Jefferson of the Servant's Home, one has to consider what took place during the Friday at the stable and coach house.

"At half-past five o'clock in the morning Barrett was seen to leave the house and go in the direction of the stable, and a little after six o'clock the witness saw a light in the stable and heard a hammering noise and some whistling. Now you have to consider what the noise was and who was the person who was there? We heard from Mr. Wolfenden earlier that Barrett alone was in charge of the premises. So who else could have been there? What did it all mean? This is for you, the jury, to decide.

"Then there are the noises heard by Mrs Kendall, the matron, and the footsteps that she heard go down the street to be accounted for. Mrs. Kendall had no interest to come forth and say that which is not true, or to make fabrications. Therefore, you need to question why all the swilling? What was the necessity for anyone to be there after twelve o'clock?

"Now, the next thing is, if Dyer is to be believed, Barrett was passing down the street with a bundle in front of him. The next question is whether this man is a reliable witness. Can you believe him? If not, then his evidence of course, means nothing. However, considering other evidence, Dyer's evidence is very important, for without it the link of circumstantial evidence is broken.

"Now, Mrs. Cooper testified earlier that she had seen a man going past the bicycle shop with a small parcel like a suit of clothes and not a parcel, like that which Dyer said. That was ten minutes after Dyer saw Barrett. So perhaps you may conclude that the parcel Mrs Cooper saw was not the same as that in which the mangled remains of the deceased were discovered.

"Now, let us look at the motive for this crime. Surely, the most outrageous crime had either been committed, or attempted upon the child by the person in whose power he had been. If that was a correct assumption, then the whole matter can then be explained.

"If you, the jury believe the evidence of Dyer, and the corroboration if there is any, and believe also first the chain of circumstances are made out, it will be your duty to return a verdict of wilful murder against Barrett. However, if you still do not find a *prima facia* case has been made, then you should return an open verdict.

"I ask you not to shrink from your duty as jurors if you feel that the verdict is in any way adverse to that of William Barrett."

The jurors retired to confer at seven o'clock, and within an hour and ten minutes of deliberation, they had reached a verdict.

"Have you reached a verdict?" asked Mr. Hutchinson?

"We have, Your Worship."

"What is your verdict, Mr. Gaskarth?"

"We did not reach a unanimous verdict, Your Worship, but with a vote of 12 to 2, we return a verdict of wilful murder against William Barrett."

The news of Barrett's impending re-arrest spread through Bradford like a flash flood, with a ripple effect that stretched beyond the fringes of the town. Large crowds soon gathered in the immediate neighbourhood of both the police station in Leeds Road and at the Midland Railway Station.

The inquest had been heard that evening just before the last train was about to leave from Bradford to Cononley where Barrett was currently living. A warrant had to be issued promptly. It was. Chief Detective-Inspector Dobson and two of his most trusted men had no sooner obtained the coroner's warrant than they were rushing off to the Midland Station in great haste to make sure that they did not miss the train.

People jostled and shouted on the station platform, many urging the police to bring Barrett to justice while others were calling for clemency and professing his innocence. Long after the train had departed, with the inspectors safely on board, people continued to gather. Even after midnight, throngs of people determinedly braved the cold February night air to vent their feelings about the case most vociferously to all who would care to listen.

It was after ten o'clock by the time the inspectors finally reached Cononley Station. As they alighted, they were almost tempted to stop for something to eat at a local pub they had passed at the bottom of Main Street, called simply, "The Railway," the reason being that none of them had eaten anything since breakfast time. However, spurred on by their sense of duty, they proceeded up Main Street in search of the house.

They found it propped up in a row of others, not three minutes from the station. Despite the late hour, the lights were still on. Dobson stepped forward and knocked rapidly several times. It was soon answered, and Sarah Metcalfe, Barrett's mother-in-law, opened the door.

"Mrs. Metcalfe?" asked Dobson.

She eyed the three men with suspicion, not opening the door fully. A slither of light shone onto the dark pavement. It gradually increased in size when she realized who they were.

"What do you want?" she asked bluntly, still not inviting them in.

"Is William Barrett home, ma'am?" they asked politely.

"Maybe. Maybe not."

"Would it be possible to discuss this indoors, Mrs. Metcalfe?" Revellers from the pub were walking home and their presence was attracting undue attention. He did not want any unpleasant scenes.

She begrudgingly stepped aside and let them in, just as Margaret came out of the kitchen with hands wet and wiping them on her apron. She looked at the three men with contempt because she recognised at least one of them. He had invaded her house in Bateman Street and had searched it from top to bottom.

"What do you lot want now, coming 'ere in the dead of night disturbing our 'ousehold? 'Aven't you caused enough trouble for us?"

Baby Nellie, rudely awoken by her mother's strident voice, let out a piercing howl.

In the front room sat her younger brother John, a strapping young man in his early twenties who had not stood up when they had entered the house. Instead, Dobson could see that he was brooding. He was clenching and unclenching his fists; spoiling for a confrontation.

Arthur Dobson stood in the middle of the room and spoke in a calm voice trying to diffuse the situation.

"We'd like to talk to your husband, Mrs. Barrett."

"For what?" she demanded.

"That's between us and Mr. Barrett. We'd prefer to talk to him about it directly."

"Well, he ain't 'ere!" she retorted triumphantly.

"Where is he?" Dobson asked patiently.

"'E's still at work. Luckily, 'e found work after you destroyed 'is chances in Bradford. Destroyed the life of an innocent man, you did! Shame on the lot of you!"

Her voice was rising, and Dobson was feeling a little uncomfortable being the target of this vitriolic attack. Baby Nellie continued to wail.

Ignoring Margaret Barrett, he directed his next question to her mother. "When are you expecting him to be home, Mrs. Metcalfe?"

Sarah Metcalfe had said nothing during her daughter's tirade. Instead, she stood with her hands on her hips, looking equally combative.

"He should be home within the hour. You might as well sit down," she said begrudgingly and gestured for them to sit.

They did so with some relief as Margaret Barrett finally left the room to attend to her screaming child.

They sat in awkward silence for nearly 30 minutes before they heard the key in the lock turn and William Barrett finally walked through the front door to his home.

As he entered the house, and before he could shut the door, the three men were on their feet.

Dobson reached into his inner coat pocket and pulled out the warrant he had been protecting since leaving Bradford. He handed it to Barrett without saying a word. Detective King moved towards the open door and stood on the threshold just in case Barrett tried to make a quick exit.

Barrett read the warrant and then looked at Chief Detective-Inspector Dobson with a strange look on his face, before he spat out, "You can't be serious!"

Dobson moved towards him. "William Barrett I am arresting you for the wilful murder of John Gill."

Suddenly all hell broke loose. The women in the house erupted with anger and John Metcalfe, who had remained silent up until then, sprung to his feet and lunged towards one of the officers. A scuffle broke out, and Dobson was losing control.

"Mr. Metcalfe, if you strike one of my officers you will be the next one in gaol!"

John Metcalfe hesitated and then thought better of it. He dropped his raised fists. However, there was a lot of weeping and consternation going on with the two women, while Barrett just stood in the room shaking his head in disbelief.

Patrons from the nearby pub had heard the commotion and had come running up the road to see what was going on. Passers-by did the same thing on hearing the shouts and raised voices. Suddenly the house was filled with angry people demanding that the police leave Barrett in peace.

"Be off with you, you low-life scum!" shouted one man, eyes hooded from the overindulgence of cheap ale. "We'll not allow you to haul our Willie off to the gaol again for nowt! Don't you have anything else to do except arrest innocent men? Now nip on back to Bradford where you belong! There's nothing for you here!" he snarled. He lunged towards Dobson, forcing Detective King to step in between them.

Dobson boomed, "Enough of this nonsense! You men clear off! We will not tolerate this obstreperous behaviour. Get yourselves home before we arrest the lot of you."

He advanced towards the main ringleader, whose friends now formed a ring around them and were looking extremely belligerent and menacing. Dobson was worried that things were getting nasty and by the looks of it, quite quickly. They were horribly outnumbered. He hoped reason would emerge the victor.

"We are here just doing our jobs, and this is none of your business! Unless you want to spend tonight in the local lock-up I suggest you all go home now to your families. Go! Now!"

The men could see that the policemen were serious, and although the policemen were outnumbered, the ale was playing tricks with their minds and bodies and perhaps it was time to go home, after all. After a few more taunts and jibes, the crowd eventually dispersed.

"Why are you arresting me again?" Barrett finally managed to ask, rooted to the floor of his front room, shocked at the news. "I've already been found not guilty by the magistrates. How's this possible?"

"Mr. Barrett, I understand that this is difficult for everyone," said Dobson, who suddenly felt timeworn and very old. "But new evidence has since been submitted, and the jury at the Coroner's Inquest has voted for you to be tried at the Assizes Court in Leeds. You will need to return with us now. Bid goodbye to your family as we need to return to Bradford as soon as possible."

"Can the man not have his evening meal, surely?" asked Sarah Metcalfe knowing that Barrett had eaten very little all day.

Dobson hesitated, and then said, "Well, ma'am, as the train does not leave for Bradford until the morning, I am sure that Mr. Barrett could stay a while longer and have something to eat before we go."

Barrett washed his hands, face in the kitchen sink, and enjoyed his last moments of freedom. While he ate his meal, he placated the womenfolk, especially his mother-in-law, who was now weeping uncontrollably. He was doing his best to reassure them that they were not to worry, as he would be all right.

While he ate, the three men, just as hungry, merely watched and wished that they were somewhere else. Anywhere, rather than being out in the cold late at night dealing with fraught women, angry townsfolk, empty bellies and parched throats.

While Barrett was eating, Dobson decided that he would not risk another public spectacle while waiting for the train at Cononley Station. He sent Detective Butterworth in search of a cab and instructed him to bring it back to the house, which he duly did within in a short time. Just as well, for as soon as they took Barrett out of the house a larger crowd had started to gather. The atmosphere was growing hostile.

Barrett said goodbye to his weeping mother-in-law, hugged his resigned wife and shook hands with his young brother-in-law before climbing into the waiting cab.

While they bounced around on the uneven road to Skipton, they sat in silence. Barrett was trying to fathom out how it was that he was in this situation, once again. The other men, desperately wanting a meal and their beds, were relieved that they had completed the mission relatively unscathed. However, it would be several hours before any of them would get to bed because the first morning train that would take them to Bradford would only arrive just before 4:00 a.m.

CHAPTER SIXTEEN – WEDNESDAY 6TH FEBRUARY 1889

Barrett was brought up in the custody of Detectives King and Butterworth at the Coroner's Court. Mr. John Craven was again representing Barrett; Mr. James Freeman was there on behalf of the Treasury and the Chief Constable for the police.

The Rev. John Whitaker, the Vicar of Cononley, was also present. He took a seat next to the witness box, just as William Barrett entered the courtroom.

The Chief Constable happened to look up from his notes that he had made when he stopped and focused his small, beady eyes on the man sitting next to Barrett. He recognised him as the vicar responsible for writing the letter to the newspaper that was now giving him heartburn, just thinking about it. He was having none of this.

He stood up, scrapping the chair on the flagstones beneath, and pointed his finger at the vicar. Those present in the courthouse immediately stopped talking. The silence was deafening. Addressing the court, he moved his finger backwards and forwards, concentrating on the vicar.

"Just let this gentleman, the Vicar of Cononley get up. I will not have him sitting here talking to Barrett during the session."

The vicar's cheeks took on a deep rose pink. He was stunned but said not a word. He politely removed himself from sitting next to Barrett and a place was hastily made so that he could sit next to the Reverend instead. Court resumed, but not before Withers noticed that as he sat down the Reverend patted the vicar's knee in a token of sympathy for the mortified man.

Mr. Hutchinson addressed William Barrett.

"Are you William Barrett?"

"Aye," was the sullen reply.

"The jury has found upon an inquisition a verdict of wilful murder against you for the murder of John Gill. It is my duty to commit you to the Armley Gaol to take your trial upon that charge, which I do now."

John Craven stood up. "May I see your warrant?"

Hutchinson raised his eyebrows at Craven, whom he was finding increasingly irksome. He handed over the warrant with a flourish, knowing that everything was in order. Craven deliberately gave it a mere superficial glance before putting it down on the table.

Craven addressed the court, trying to justify his actions. "I am anxious only that the duties of the Bradford police should be known. Barrett surrenders himself today and he is eager to be removed to Armley Gaol at once."

Nothing of what Craven had just said made any difference to the court. It had the authority to hold Barrett for as long as possible, whenever they pleased, wherever they pleased. Craven knew that, but he was anxious for Barrett, as he knew that it could be months before the trial came before the Assizes in Leeds.

The court held all the aces.

Mr. Hutchinson was well aware of the situation and this time he was not going to allow the young whippersnapper Craven to get the upper hand. He replied airily, "I shall issue the commitment in due course."

"That means today, sir," insisted Craven.

Hutchinson was not amused. He leaned forward, with folded arms and stared at Craven. Moments passed. Tensions heightened. Silence flooded the room.

"I said that it will be done as soon as it can be done, Mr. Craven. Is that now understood?" He watched, to his great satisfaction as Craven visibly squirmed.

Hutchinson then turned to the police, and with a dismissive movement of his hand he said, "You can take him away now."

Barrett, pale but composed, was removed from the courtroom while John Craven remained where he was.

CHAPTER SEVENTEEN – TUESDAY 12TH FEBRUARY 1889

If Barrett had known of the appalling conditions held within the walls of the "big house on the hill," as Armley Gaol was fondly called by the locals, he may not have been so keen to get there.

It certainly was not anything like the conditions he had experienced in Bradford. There he had been able to chat to the police officers quite amicably and had been generally well looked after. Armley was going to be an entirely different experience.

He had travelled from Bradford sandwiched between Detective Butterworth and King, whose duty it had been on the Thursday last to deliver him safely to the gaol in Leeds. It had been a day of inclement weather; rain falling intermittently with sunshine scarce. As they approached the town, the dark battlements of the gaol dominated the skyline. Before them, was an extensive and rather oppressive looking stone fortress. It was castellated with round turrets and tall, outer walls. As they got closer, Barrett noticed how the walls were black with smog and grime, only adding to the feeling of bleakness and austerity.

Now he found himself incarcerated for twenty-three hours out of every twenty-four. The remaining precious hour he spent walking around the circular pathways of the exercise yard monitored by two burly guards to whom he was not allowed to talk. Therefore, it came about that he cultivated the company of a rat.

The rat first appeared in his cell during meal times. It seemed to sense when food would be about. Just before the allotted time it would sit in the corner closest to the door cleaning its whiskers and waiting patiently for him to toss it something to eat. During the first few days, Barrett had hurled his stale bread crusts at it, with good aim, while he ate his meagre daily ration of cheese and bread. Despite hitting it several times a day, it persisted in coming back.

As the days went by, with no other company, he found himself actively feeding it and looking forward to its visits. Once the quality of Barrett's meals had improved, after he began receiving food from outside the prison walls, the rat had fast become a regular visitor.

It certainly helped break the monotony. Day after day, he had nothing else to do other than to lie full-length and stretched out on the narrow bed covered with a thin, filthy blanket. Gripping the cast iron bedstead with both hands behind his head, it was here that he did a lot of thinking. The whitewashed ceiling with the amorphic brown rosettes of water stains and mildew spots were becoming vaguely familiar to him.

His eyes were bloodshot through lack of sleep and they felt sandy and sore. The first reason being that his pillow was thin and hard. It was decidedly uncomfortable. The second was because his bed crawled with lice. He had welts all over his legs and stomach from where he they had bitten him during the night. While he scratched his bites in the dark, he listened to the shouts of his fellow inmates. People he would never see.

One night he had had a very bad night. He came out of a deep sleep when he felt the weight of someone sitting on the edge of his bed. Suddenly, he was wide awake. He lay on the small bed in the blackness of the night and sensed a sudden draught. There it was again. He felt the bed move with the weight of someone suddenly shifting, coming closer. He lay there wondering who it could be when an icy breath, devoid of human warmth, skimmed his cheek. The hairs on the back of his neck bristled.

He sat bolt upright and sprung out of bed. He struck a match to light the candle but his hands were trembling and he fumbled with the match several times. As soon as the wick finally caught, the flame went out. After a while, he managed to get the candle lit. He took the waxen stump and holding it outwards with an outstretched arm, moved it around his small cell.

The pale yellow light fell onto the bed. It was empty, save for the chamber pot beneath it. He moved the candle around in a slow arc, pivoting his feet in a tight circle, his hand still trembling. The light found the small wooden table opposite the bed carved with the initials of past prisoners. On top of that, he could see his pewter mug and plate. He completed the circle and came back to the bed. There was nothing there. After a long while, he blew out the candle, crawled back under the lice-infested blanket to keep warm in the dank, damp cell and slept fitfully for the rest of the night.

He mentioned the incident the following morning to the prison guard who had just brought him his breakfast.

"There are lots of ghosts here in Armley, son. You just make sure you don't end up becoming one of them!" He laughed heartily at his own joke, and then conceded, "Sounds like old Charlie Pearce has been up to his old tricks." With no more of an explanation, he slopped out some thin gruel to the next prisoner who clearly did not have thoughtful friends like Barrett.

The guard backtracked and came back to Barrett.

"Ah, Barrett, I forgot. This was delivered this morning." He passed William Barrett an unopened envelope addressed to him at the gaol. He opened it straightaway, thinking it was a letter from his lawyer. It was not.

'Dear Billy,

'I write to tell you that things are looking awfully black against you in Bradford, and you had better confess that you did it. Remember this, Billy, even if you do get off, you will surely be stabbed to death, because there are two men, who are dead against you, and they have sworn to avenge that poor little boy's death which you so cruelly took and murdered in that horrible way.

'Oh God help you to confess, Billy. Oh Billy, there will be no peace for you again on this miserable earth. Even if you get off, because wherever you go you will be pointed at. Billy, make it all clear, for as sure as God is in heaven, you did it.

'Oh, Billy, remember that poor little lamb's blood is crying to heaven for vengeance this very minute, and I know you can hear his cry. There is no chance for you, Billy. Only this, perhaps you may be said to be wrong in your head but you are not, are you Billy?

'Oh do confess your guilty heart to God and make your peace with him on this earth before you are lost. Billy, you often told me that there was no God, but Oh Billy, there is and he is looking into your guilty heart just now and he is ready to forgive you your horrible sins, Billy. Remember, Billy what I used to tell you? "Him that cometh to me I will in no wise cast out - come unto me all ye that are heavy laden and I will give you rest, ask and thou shalt receive, seek and ye shall find, knock and it shall be opened unto you."

Billy, you remember me telling you all these. Billy? See how useful to you they are now? You won't laugh at them now Billy they are just fit for you now.

'I have posted this in Bradford because I dare not post it at home as they would know me in a minute and I don't want to be brought against you Billy after knowing you so long. Oh Billy, confess and you can yet be pardoned by Almighty God. Do Billy go down on your knees when you read my poor letter and confess all, and get your sins washed away in the sight of God. Never mind what people say. Look to your only hope; God. Billy, are you not afraid God will smite your black lying heart if you do not confess? Remember you can never prosper. You will be, and are, the same as Cain with God's mark on his forehead. Think of all this Billy.

'Oh Billy ask for forgiveness from your heavenly Father on high and you will be saved from Hell and everlasting damnation.

'Oh Billy, think of your poor Margaret. She is your wife and she is nearly mad. But you know Billy, she can never love you the same again. She would always be afraid of you if even you get off. But if you do, you will be killed. Oh, Billy, I could not help writing this poor letter to you because I do not want the Devil to get you. I want you to go to Heaven out of this wicked world. Oh Billy, ask God's pardon just now pray earnestly Billy. I need not put my name I wrote on Sunday last.

'Billy God bless you.'

The letter disturbed Barrett. He folded it up and put it in his pocket. He tried to think who it was from. There was a niggle in the back of his mind, and it remained there. He kept it to show his lawyer.

He was hoping to hear from his lawyer later in the morning. He had had a meeting with John Craven a few days prior, and he had promised Barrett that he would apply for bail and get him out of this hell hole fairly soon. He was hoping that it would be today that he would hear some good news.

However, Craven did not come, instead he was passed a note by another guard later during the day.

Barrett sat on the edge of his bed opened it and read it slowly.

'Dear Mr. Barrett -

'It is with regret that I inform you that your application for bail, made by my esteemed colleague Mr. Samuel Danks Waddy, Q.C., M.P. on behalf of my law firm, was rejected by the Treasury yesterday, due to a strong protest made by Mr. Freeman. 'Despite the fact that we said that if bail were to be made, we were prepared to pay a substantial amount, unfortunately, Freeman had the judge's ear.

'There is little chance now that you will be released before your trial. I am very sorry.

'Yours truly, John W. Craven.'

William Barrett put the letter aside on the table, lay down on the narrow bed, and contemplated the ceiling rosettes, once again.

CHAPTER EIGHTEEN – MONDAY 11TH - TUESDAY 12TH MARCH 1889

William Barrett had spent almost a month in the Almery Gaol before his case came up before the Leeds Assizes. Despite the long wait, he and his lawyers were feeling confident about the outcome of the case. Craven had repeatedly told him that he would get the case dismissed, as all the evidence presented was purely speculative.

Yesterday, the case before the Grand Jury had dragged on for more than four hours. Witness after witness took to the stand telling the court what they had seen, or thought they had seen. All of which Barrett had heard several times over.

Shadows were long before the jury finally had their decision.

The foreman of the Grand Jury rose, and Barrett again felt the tension course through his veins. He stood waiting for his future to be decided by a handful of men; his life hinged on a vote.

The foreman cleared his throat, and a hush fell over the crowded courthouse.

"In this case, we have been unable to examine three witnesses, but none of them do we consider material. I say this wishing to explain why they were not called. They were not in attendance due to illness or other causes. Every other witness we have examined."

He then handed a piece of paper to His Lordship's Clerk, who in turn, passed it to the Court Commissioner who then read the contents out aloud.

"We, the members of the Grand Jury, find no true bill against William Barrett for murder."

A muffled hum of exclamations went around the courtroom, and an outbreak of applause soon followed.

"Order! Order!"

Barrett exhaled and smiled. The euphoria was short lived.

"Mr. Barrett, although this court has not found you guilty, you are still to be detained due to the case on the coroner's verdict. You will need to appear in this court again shortly so that your fate can finally be decided."

Barrett's life had been one long cycle of hope and despair. He had forgotten about the Coroner's Inquest and was expecting that this case would be the deciding one. He felt numb as he returned to his cell. While he was being moved he could hear the shouts of encouragement from those outside. His spirits soared, albeit briefly.

Tuesday dawned, and William Barrett was hoping that this case would finally go away. When court reconvened, he was not allowed into the courtroom, but his lawyers, Mr. Waddy and John Craven, were still representing him. Mr. Forbes Q.C. represented the prosecution and the treasury. Mr. Forbes now rose to address the court.

"Gentlemen of the court, the Grand Jury has thrown out the bill against William Barrett and under the circumstances I, and those who have instructed me, feel that it would be useless to proceed on the verdict of the Coroner's Inquisition.

"The question is, however, what is to be done in this case?

"The evidence, such as it is, is entirely of suspicion. The learned counsel proceeding points out that there are but three alternatives open to the prosecution.

"The first course would be to apply to the Attorney General for a writ of *nolle prosequs*. Under this, the prosecution could set aside the Coroner's Inquisition, and in case any fresh evidence was found, the prisoner could again be brought up and charged with the offence.

"The second course is to offer no evidence at all but to allow the prisoner to be set at liberty.

"The third course would be to allow the prisoner to put upon his trial, to have the usual proclamation read, and to offer no evidence.

"We ask our learned Commissioner, Mr. Frederick Meadows White of the Queen's Council, to accept the responsibility of saying upon which of the alternatives the prosecution should act."

"In my reply," the Commissioner said, "I would like to consult with Mr. Justice Denman as to the appropriate course to take."

Samuel Waddy, his grey hair swept high off his forehead, stroked his bushy and lustrous grey beard and adjusted his round, steel-rimmed glasses that were in the habit of sliding down his aquiline nose.

He rose and said, "If I may, Your Lordship. I believe that the invariable course in this circuit has been that when the Grand Jury has indicated its view as clearly as it has done in this case, then a verdict of 'Not Guilty' should be taken on the Coroner's Inquisition. In my long experience, I do not think that there have ever been any exceptions to this. I feel that in this particular instance any departure from the ordinary course would be exceedingly painful.

"I do not wish to say anything reflecting upon the Coroner's Court, but as a matter of fact at the coroner's jury certain important witnesses were not called who had already been called before the magistrates, and upon whose evidence the magistrates had resolved that there was no case against Barrett. The coroner's jury had not examined two or three of the principal witnesses, but in my opinion, sir, they had come to a hasty conclusion.

"Now, in mercy and justice, Barrett after being cleared by the magistrates, and by the Grand Jury, should not because of a coroner's jury, acting on partial information, come to an unfortunate conclusion, be dragged before the court to be tried for murder. I think that a situation such as that would be worse than death, and I entreat Your Lordship, to take the course invariably taken in such cases.

"However if any human being be found to prefer an accusation against the man's character, then let him do it now, for the man was prepared to take his trial, and to meet any charge preferred against him."

After this long and impassioned discourse, Mr. Waddy took to his seat.

The commissioner then replied, "I personally have a strong opinion on the matter, but I still think that under the peculiar circumstances in which I am placed, that it would still only be right to consult Justice Denman. I suggest we adjourn for lunch."

After lunch the esteemed commissioner, Frederick Meadows White, was still in a quandary and was still not able to conclude the case.

"I have consulted with Mr. Justice Denman and have concluded that it is not my duty to give an opinion as to what course the prosecution should take in the Barrett case."

His overt indecisiveness in the ruling that all were counting on, gave the prosecution team the opportunity they had been looking for. Mr. Forbes now rose.

"Perhaps, Your Lordship, I may have the opportunity of communicating with the Attorney-General, who may want to proceed on the Coroner's Inquisition?"

Mr. Waddy rose to his feet as quickly as his aging frame allowed.

"Sir! Asking the Attorney-General to proceed on the Coroner's Inquisition is unheard of!" he said in protest. "Mr. Barrett should be allowed to plead."

"Your Lordship, if it helps any, the additional evidence we the Treasury have obtained is, in fact, more favourable to the prisoner than unfavourable. If the prisoner were to be put on trial now, the prosecution would not tender evidence," conceded Mr. Forbes.

"Where is the prisoner?" asked the commissioner.

"The prisoner is awaiting trial in his cell, Your Lordship," explained Mr. Waddy.

"Bring the prisoner up to the dock, then."

The strain of the case was telling on Barrett. He walked into the courtroom a man changed from a few months prior; one who had been deprived of his freedom, one who now appreciated the value of liberty.

"How do you plead, Mr. Barrett?"

"Not guilty, sir," he said in a firm voice.

"You will be detained for an arraignment later," replied the commissioner.

Within the hour, Barrett came back into the dock, and was re-arraigned.

Mr. Forbes addressed the commissioner. "Your Lordship, on behalf of the prosecution in this case, I propose to offer no evidence against the prisoner."

Frederick Meadows White deliberately addressed the jury in such a weak voice that only the jury members could hear him. He did not intend to allow the public, or the journalists present, to get wind of what he was saying. As a result, the Grand Jury members half-leaned, half-knelt on the row of seats for counsel in order to hear what was being said.

"Members of the Jury, I would like you to deliberate very carefully on this most difficult case. William Barrett has been charged with the murder and mutilation of John Gill, not quite eight.

"It is indeed a heinous crime that has been much discussed in the local newspapers and received much attention from the public. I ask that you dismiss these considerations from your mind, and concentrate merely on the evidence presented to you.

"It would seem a witness named Dyer was called before the coroner, who did not appear before the magistrates, and his testimony advanced the case against Barrett to some extent. When the case came before you, I recommended to you to watch carefully the evidence of Dyer, in order that you may see the character of the witness. And I remind you of that now.

"This case has been entirely one of circumstantial evidence, and if the Grand Jury is satisfied, the charge against Barrett is only one of suspicion, no matter how grave that suspicion may be, which does not justify a true bill. In this case, I advise you, gentlemen that it would be your duty to return a no bill. However, if you feel that the evidence presented amounts to a *prima facie* case, then of course, a true bill must be returned.

"It is not my duty to express my opinion one way or the other as to the guilt of the prisoner. I am merely asking you to give the evidence, not only that of Dyer but also that of the other witnesses, your most careful consideration."

The foreman of the jury nodded his head in agreement and Barrett, still managing to retain his composure, was again removed to the cells.

The Grand Jury spent hours deliberating the case, but they had finally reached a conclusion.

A few minutes later John Craven, who had been beside himself with the court's antics removed himself from the court and made his way to the cells. He found Barrett pacing his cell. Craven put out his hand and shook Barrett's warmly.

"Congratulations, Barrett! You are finally a free man!"

By the time Craven had reached the cells news of William Barrett's acquittal had reached the crowds milling outside the building. Cheers and shouts drifted through the bars and numbers soon swelled, all wanting to get a glimpse of the prisoner being released.

Relief had washed over William Barrett when he heard the news he had been waiting for. He was finally a free man. He would never again stand trial for the murder of John Gill. His relief was elevated to euphoria.

Not wanting to remain in gaol a minute more than needed, he took his few possessions, and with the help of the Town Hall Gaoler, Inspector Dalton, he and John Craven slipped quietly out of the building, out of a side gate near Oxford Street, and made for the Midland Station in a waiting cab.

Those who wanted to see and congratulate the man who had dominated the newspapers for the last three months had been thwarted. Not a single member of the general public witnessed his release.

CHAPTER NINETEEN – SATURDAY 16TH MARCH 1889

William Barrett was free. However, it had come at great expense, and not just personal. His solicitors, Weatherhead & Burr, had lost no time in sending out their account. The amount was significant. The case had taken far longer than anticipated and time was money, money that the Barrett family did not have, and nor did their most staunch supporters.

In order to pay these mounting defence fees they needed continued public assistance in the form of monetary contributions to go towards the Barrett Defence Fund that the local vicar had set up some time ago. Although contributions trickled through in the beginning, they had soon dried up. To re-encourage the public to part with their hard-earned pennies many activities, suppers, and dances were planned for that weekend. They would take place in the small villages and hamlets clustered around the area where Barrett was born and raised.

William Barrett and his friends left Bradford on Saturday morning by train reaching Farnhill, where flyers of his proposed visit had already been posted throughout the neighbourhood. It was hoped that these would be an effective way of attracting the crowds. It was.

Enthusiasm abounded. In the areas of Colne and Nelson, groups of people gathered in large numbers to show their support. William Barrett; his mother, now Mrs. Cooper; his brother-in-law John Metcalfe; Mr. John Procter Wolfenden; the Reverend J. Ashborne of Skipton;

Mr. Haswell of Kildwick; Mr. Waddington of Cross Hills; and other ladies and gentlemen were out in full force visiting the district in the hopes of enlisting their sympathies and support. Their aim was to gather large donations that would go towards the 'Fund.' It turned out to be a rather spectacular event.

When the train pulled into Kildwick Station, both the platform and the entrance to the station were thick with thronging crowds shoulder-to-shoulder, mobbing and cheering Barrett and his friends as they alighted. People slapped him on the back, while others pumped his hand, until he was finally able to free himself from the adoring crowds to join his friends in a waiting cab. They made their way to Kildwick to see the rest of his friends and family, especially his wife and child, whom he had not seen in over a month.

At Kildwick, the party first proceeded to Mr. Wolfenden's house, where they stayed for a brief time. After that, they left for Barr Hill to visit his wife, who was staying with her brother. Before they had even entered the village, loud cheers came from hordes of supporters as soon as he approached. Inside the village, more welcoming gestures were evident with several flags flying, including a large banner that spanned the main street with the inscription, 'Welcome Home.'

After a short delay at Barr Hill, the party then proceeded to Cononley by train, accompanied by a multitude of people who ran behind his cab.

When leaving the station they gave him the perfect ovation. He was, for a considerable distance, carried shoulder high. It seemed that the enthusiasm of the people knew no bounds. When they saw him off, as the train was pulling out the station one could still hear, above the clickety-clack of the iron wheels on the tracks and the hissing of the steam of the engine, resounding shouts of what a good fellow he was.

When they arrived at Cononley, no smaller crowd was there to receive him. A small pony phaeton was then requisitioned in which were seated Barrett, Mr. Whitaker the vicar, Mr. Wolfenden, and Mr. Cardwell. Many willing hands dragged along the vehicle while the Farnhill Band preceded the phaeton playing, 'See the Conquering Hero Comes.'

In addition, such a display of buntings that one had never before seen in Cononley. Almost every house had a flag, and whole lines of flags stretched across the streets. At the centre of the village a specially built triumphal arch bearing the words, 'Welcome Home' had been erected for this momentous and auspicious occasion.

Prominent, in this very public display, was an effigy of Chief Constable Withers dressed in a policeman's coat and hanging by the neck in the market square. He was raised and lowered countless times to the jeers of "Owd Withers!"

The end of the day ended on a high with a small dinner and dance. During the evening the Barrett family and their supporters were already refining their plans for the following day. Cononley was chosen as the place where the procession would start next, due to his strong connections there.

The Farnhill band was still playing long into the night, and this time they were playing some dance music. The young people needed no excuse to indulge in a little dancing to conclude such a festive and momentous occasion.

On Sunday, a large number of mounted farmers attended all wagons, carriages, farmer's gigs and carts loaded with human freight, drawn by horses gaily decorated. They drove from Cononley along the turnpike to Kildwick, the Junction, Eastburn, Sutton, Cross Hills, Glusburn and Cowling.

Barrett rode prominently at the head of this vast procession on horseback, all the while smiling, waving, and bending down from time to time to shake hands with his supporters who lined the way.

Inhabitants, excited by the unusual procession, the pomp and ceremony that broke the monotony of their boring lives, assembled eagerly in each village. Whether they knew who he was, or what had happened to him, remains unknown. However, there was a lot of cheering indicating that he was clearly the hero of the day.

They halted in an open space at the bridge near Cononley, ironically called Hen Gill Bridge. Here the Reverend Whitaker addressed the assembly. At the end of it, he announced that he had persuaded Barrett to say a few words. Tumultuous applause erupted, soon followed by an awkward pause. No words came forth from Barrett who remained firmly rooted to his seat. After a brief consultation, Mr. Wolfenden rose and said that Barrett was so deeply affected that he felt it impossible to say anything. People dispersed feeling deeply disappointed.

At each halting place, they collected offerings from the sympathetic. The Reverend Tack, a member of the Primitive Methodist and who had, along with the Vicar of Cononley, taken an active interest in Barrett's welfare. He now addressed a few appropriate words to a new assembly.

They then stopped at the Free Trade Hall, also packed with an enthusiastic audience. Mr. Wolfenden stood up and spoke passionately to those who were there. He detailed the evidence given against Barrett at the recent trial.

"The police deliberately held back certain information that was favourable to Barrett. For example, the testimony of James Head, who had seen the boy John Gill leave Barrett on the morning of the murder and heard him say, 'I will go for my breakfast,' was never heard!

"The case was, in my opinion, badly managed by the police force from beginning to end! And, the only result of their persistent efforts was to incriminate Barrett because it was easy to do so! The police have been licked with their own whips as not a single witness for the defence had to be called!"

He ended his speech triumphantly to a thunderous applause with many shouting, 'Hear! Hear!

Mr. Hartley moved a resolution congratulating Barrett on his acquittal and sympathised with him during the trial he had undergone.

"I have always believed in Barrett's innocence. If I had taken any part of the proceedings against Barrett, I should never have been able to forgive myself. As for the police, I do not know what manner of men they are, or how they can reconcile their conduct."

He sat down and more applause followed.

Mr. John Riley seconded the motion, and the resolution was carried with much acclamation.

The Reverend Osborne, Barrett's pastor, then addressed the meeting and testified to Barrett's good character. He laid stress upon the mental suffering endured by Barrett during his incarceration in Armley Gaol. He also mentioned that £550 had been the cost of the defence and he appealed to those that were there to assist in clearing the debt.

Although people had voted with a show of appearance, they had not done so with their generosity. Only £11.00 had been raised to date.

Rain unfortunately interfered with the complete success of the procession. However, provision for tea had been made at two of the public schools for a thousand people and private resources were being heavily taxed.

One could say that, overall, the public meeting had been largely successful, with a large attendance despite the weather, and the proceedings of the day would no doubt help to go towards the £550 legal bill that the Barrett family was facing.

That evening celebrations concluded in Cononley after a tiring day of more meetings and greetings, with a supper held in the Old Fellow's Hall, where they managed to raise additional funds.

The Leeds Times on 16th March had the following to say about the case.

'The Manningham tragedy remains enveloped in mystery. Never has the mistaken policy of the provincial police force been more fully demonstrated than in connection with this painful and horrible crime.

'The extraordinary tenacity with which the local police clung to the theory respecting the suspected milkman, Barrett, and neglected to look around for other clues in the earlier stages of the case, merits, and is receiving, the severest possible public condemnation.

'It will be remembered that the magistrates who conducted the preliminary inquiry repeatedly commented on the fact that the time of the court was being wasted with hearing certain statements which, even as an apology for evidence, were utterly worthless. The case against Barrett had never a single element of substantiality about it, and the magistrates for once showed that they had the courage of their convictions by dismissing the charge, and setting the prisoner free.

'The action of the magistrates was approved of by the public at the time - with the result that the suspected murderer who had been dismissed without the slightest stain on his character,

and practically proclaimed as innocent as the dead or the unborn, was for the nonce, made a martyr.

'Concerts and entertainments of various kinds were held in his honour; sermons were preached in vindication of the spotless purity of his character; the magistrates were applauded for the courageous part they had played...'

William Barrett's court case and his final release had overshadowed the memory of John Gill. The press overlooked his devastated parents, Thomas and Mary Ann Gill. Other than their initial interviews soon after the murder, they were no longer seen as newsworthy and were never interviewed again.

The Gills were never asked how they were coping, how they viewed the proceedings, Barrett's exoneration, or even whether they felt the police had arrested the right person. The focus had always been on William Barrett, who had dominated centre stage; finally hailed as a hero, a saint, and a martyr.

One wonders what the Gills would have said.

If only they had been asked.

AFTERWORD

The sad story of John Gill is based on actual facts and events. No names or places were changed and everything you have read about took place, as reported.

I took licence to humanize the events and to bring these characters to life. I tried very hard to tell the story as an impartial bystander and to allow you to draw your own conclusions as to who killed Johnny Gill. In my journey, however, I found it very hard to remain impartial.

There were many people, including those still today, who believe that Withers was too hasty in his choice of a suspect. That he had had 'tunnel vision' concerning William Barrett, allowing the real perpetrator to go free. Many believed in his innocence.

Others felt that it had been the work of the same person who was responsible for the East London murders. The letters portending that Jack the Ripper had been up to Bradford and 'torn up a little boy' are said, by some, to have been two of the few genuine letters of the time. The argument being that the displacement of the organs, and the draping of the intestines and positioning of the heart mirrored the murder of Mary Jane Kelly. Some will also say that each of the prostitutes who were killed had some sort of neckwear found at the crime scenes, and so the white shirting placed on John Gill was an important signature of Jack the Ripper.

Others felt that they needed to look closer to home. Members of the recently formed occult chapter of the Golden Dawn also fell under suspicion. Was John Gill murdered as part of a ritualistic killing? The date of his murder had not gone unnoticed.

While researching this extremely convoluted story, I set out with an open mind as to whether William Barrett was guilty or not. I have to be honest: I wavered several times. In the end, I was convinced that no one else was responsible. William Barrett had committed the perfect murder. It is, of course, only my opinion.

From my perspective, William Barrett, in today's world, would have been labelled the classic sociopath. Although always a man of few words when he chose, it was not what he said or what he did not say that highlights him as such. It was what he did, or did not do, that were the classic tell-tale signs.

His outward persona was that of a charming man, fooling many by being selective in which side his character he wished to show. I saw him as scheming and cunning. He was clever, manipulative, and deadly. The man who never drank in front of his employer was drunk on duty. There were those who had seen him viciously strike out at animals; but vehemently denied by others. Those who had seen his bad temper, were cancelled out by those who could attest to his sweet nature.

His sociopathic tendencies were numerable. He displayed no empathy for the Gills. Nor did he show any emotion or sadness for the loss of the boy, a boy who was supposed to have been his little friend and companion. He displayed odd and inappropriate behaviour while incarcerated, showing no appreciation for the severity of the position he was in. Instead, he was singing, joking, laughing, and behaving in an upbeat manner.

More importantly, he was so full of his own sense of grandiose importance that he showed no natural nervousness that any other person would have displayed if placed in the same position. Moreover, he continued to do so right through to the end of his trial.

Another highly suspicious situation was that despite his outward show of concern he had not once offered to search for the boy. Instead, he had boldly knocked on their door on the pretext of concern in asking about his whereabouts. This was deliberate, so that he could make sure that the courts knew this very early on in the case. When he got the chance, he did tell the courts, very loudly. Again, this is manipulative behaviour.

When the men at the cabstand were talking about the boy's disappearance, he did not, as far as we know, take part in the conversation. Why not? Only if you are guilty, and you decide that it is best to say nothing, so that you do not draw too much attention to yourself. However, the opposite effect occurred. By not saying anything, people became rightly suspicious.

Barrett could read and write, and openly said that the Jack the Ripper cases had intrigued and affected him greatly. I believe, too, that he had read how evidence could be obliterated in previous murder cases, and he had set out to do just that after killing John Gill. Arthur Conan Doyle was a contemporary author, ahead of his time with his thoughts on Forensic Science that he wove into his stories. It is a pity that no one checked the library to see what books Barrett had read prior to the murder.

What was the motive?

We will never know, but I believe that the gossip that was spread by John Gill, which destroyed the picture of the perfect man he liked to portray to many, was his undoing.

There are two scenarios. The first one is that he did not plan to kill the boy. He was angry with Johnny for spreading the story of him being drunk on duty, and perhaps he had words with the boy during the round and had killed him in a blind rage by accident, more than likely at the stables.

Not knowing what to do with the body he hid it under straw in the storage part of the stable, resumed his round, and then dismembered it later over the next two nights make it to look like the work of Jack the Ripper, whom he had recently read about. The body could have been wrapped up in the coarse wrapper, away from prying eyes. Because it was winter, there would have been little decomposition and therefore no smell of death.

The fact that he smelled of rum and was agitated during the round can now be explained. Having killed the boy, he would have been agitated and had probably had several stiff drinks before he was able to resume the round and pretend normality. He had also access to water where he washed his clothes to get rid of the blood, but blamed the rain.

The second scenario is more complex; that the motive was sexual and premeditated. Johnny had already told his mother that there had been an incident where Barrett had behaved inappropriately towards him. Unfortunately, child molestation was not well reported in those days, and the Gills were simple folk who did not go on to question their son. Had they done so, his sojourns with the milkman may well have been stopped altogether.

If Barrett had been a paedophile, his choice of career as a milkman, taking relatively poor children on his rounds, allowed him easy access. Being a Sunday school teacher was another area in his life where he had accessibility to a large number of children in his care that would have trusted him.

Forensic Science was in its infancy within the police force. Although Withers had noted semen stains on Barrett's trousers, which had prompted him to label Barrett as a man who had uncontrollable 'animal passions,' no further links were made between this evidence, the nature of the crime, and the motive.

However, perhaps the murder was not committed just so that he could have sex with the boy. It was an expression of dominance, of punishment for what he had done to Barrett through his innocent gossip.

Therefore, we come back to why Johnny Gill lost his life. Barrett would have been furious with the child for destroying the image of the upright, sober man that he had liked to portray to his employer, Wolfenden, and others, and which was not the same character that Johnny Gill had witnessed. The fact that the child had happily shared this personally embarrassing incident with the neighbourhood would have infuriated Barrett on many different levels. We know from Mary Ann that he had been most displeased with Johnny for spreading the story.

Johnny Gill was stabbed in great anger. The knife had smashed bones on entry. The killer had used such force that Doctor Lodge had likened it to having been strong enough to 'kill an elephant.' This murder had been very personal.

If this was a premeditated murder, Barrett possibly knew that the Cahills would be away on the Wednesday night and had used their house, just five or six minutes away from Manningham Lane dairy, to set the stage for the copycat Jack the Ripper murder. We know he carried a pencil in his pocket to write in his milk books, and the card left at the Cahills had been written in pencil, not ink. Pre-written, we are not sure, but there was a pen and some ink nearby that was not used. Other Jack the Ripper notes and letters, hoax or otherwise, had all been written in ink. Handwriting analysis was not yet part of Forensic Science at that stage and so a comparative handwriting study was never done.

It is also interesting that the rum smelt on Barrett's breath was the same type of alcohol missing from the Cahill household that had been stolen the previous day.

Was 9:30 marked on the clock referring to the time that John Gill would lose his life?

The greatest tragedy of this case was that the key witness for the prosecution was a simpleton, in Dyer. Had it been anyone else, Barrett would have swung. He was the lynchpin to the case. However, the Devil looks after his own, and he was certainly looking after Barrett the day Dyer came upon him and no one else who would have been a more credible witness. In addition, a crucial error made by James Withers in this case was that he had not used Dyer, his primary material witness, during the Magistrate's Inquest. This had helped secure an acquittal for Barrett before the Grand Jury in Leeds.

The final speech by Frederick Meadows White before the Assizes did not sum up the evidence in a systematic and objective manner. Instead, he presented the case in a very subjective manner that in the end swayed the jury. It was a very different summation to that given by Mr. James Gwynne Hutchinson at the end of the Coroner's Inquest.

In the end, all the evidence was circumstantial. However, there were so many circumstances that, when added up, they revealed the whole. It overwhelmingly showed a picture of guilt.

Barrett remained a free man, going on with his life to become a farm owner and finally a farm bailiff. From a lowly farm labourer, to milkman, to farm owner, to bailiff during a period of history where it was most unusual to have such a meteoric rise in one's choice of profession, is significantly interesting. One has to wonder, along with all the strong support that he got during and after the trial, that perhaps there were more important people involved in this case than we know about.

Barrett fathered four children with his wife Margaret. His eldest daughter, Nellie died at the age of twelve, and he lost another child at a young age. The cause of deaths is unknown, but I presume they were natural.

As far as I know, Barrett remained out of the sights of the law after this. However, this was an era where street urchins disappeared off the streets daily, never missed, never reported. If Barrett was guilty of murdering John Gill, there is a strong chance that there were others before, and after, the murder of young Johnny.

After the murder of their beloved son, Mary Ann and Thomas Gill were broken people. They never fully recovered from his death and they had no more children. Both girls married and had families of their own, and young Samuel became a butcher.

Thomas died many years before Mary Ann, in November 1909 at the age of 54, taken to his grave far too soon, probably brought on by stress and intense grief. Mary Ann visited Johnny's grave in the Windhill Cemetery on Owlet Road every Saturday for forty-four years, until her own death at the age of 76, in June 1932. When she died, it was fitting that she was buried in the same grave as her son, Johnny and her husband, Thomas.

No one was ever charged with the murder of young Johnny Gill.

DID YOU ENJOY THE BOOK?

If you enjoyed reading this book, please consider **leaving a review on the Amazon website**, under my sale's page. Reviews are incredibly important to authors, and I would appreciate your support. I read every review and do hope to see yours too. Here is the link:

<u>Review Page</u>

If you would like to listen to the first 40 minutes of the **audio book** for **FREE** please visit
www.kathrynmcmaster.com

I am currently writing my second book covering the story of Madeleine Smith who was accused of poisoning her lover in 1857. Did she kill him or did he end up inadvertently killing himself and if so, how and why?

Printed in Great Britain
by Amazon